WAITING TO FORGET

Waiting to Forget

Sheila Kelly Welch

namelos
South Hampton, New Hampshire

Library of Congress Control Number: 2011929425

ISBN 978-1-60898-114-4 (hardcover : alk. paper)
ISBN 978-1-60898-115-1 (pbk. : alk. paper)
ISBN 978-1-60898-116-8 (ebk.)

namelos
www.namelos.com

*To my brother, Hugh, and my sister, Shaune,
with admiration and love*

WAITING TO FORGET

1

T.J. sits, his head leaning to one side. His neck hurts. Despite three inches of padding, the chair seat is stiff and unyielding. His eyes feel gritty, as if he's been playing in a sandbox and someone threw a fistful at his face. But he hasn't been near a sandbox for years and years. Not since that blue foster home with all those cats.

Playing in cat-dirtied sand would be better than sitting in a waiting room at a hospital, T.J. thinks. He blinks twice, then lets his gaze drift, touching lightly on each person slumped in a chair.

A thin, dark woman with her hand wrapped in a towel.

A blank-faced teenager holding a snuffling baby in her arms.

A small boy, his anxious mother beside him. The boy has a cough that sounds like one of those cats getting ready to throw up.

The air smells like disinfectant combined with air freshener.

He lets his focus settle on his own hands. They grip a large book in his lap. He lifts his left hand and begins to chew his nails methodically, starting with his pinkie and ending with his thumb, until his teeth can't snip off any more. It takes a long time.

He is avoiding looking at those people again. They're all waiting to be admitted through the wide, swinging doors where Marlene and Dan already went to see his little sister, Angela, who arrived just ahead of them. In an ambulance.

He was told to wait. That's what he's been doing.

—

T.J. chews the fingernails of his right hand while he remembers their arrival at the ER.

"Wait here," Dan said with gruff authority as he hurried away.

Marlene, one step behind Dan, looked back at T.J., her eyes wet and unfocused. Her lips parted slightly as if she was about to say something, but the doors opened automatically, and she scurried through. Then the doors shut, swallowing the two of them. Leaving T.J. to wait.

That was a long time ago. T.J. lifts his eyes and tries to locate a clock, but he can't find one. He has no watch. He accidentally broke the one they bought for him. "I'm sorry, Timothy." That's what Dan said. "When you're older and more responsible, we'll get you another one."

Dan often talks to T.J. about being more careful, more responsible. Most of the kids in his seventh-grade class at Levinburgh Middle School have watches, and cell phones, too. They must be lots more responsible, T.J. thinks. Probably they don't ever take off their watches and leave them on the bedroom floor and then accidentally tramp on them, smashing the glass—or was it plastic?—and making the glowing numerals disappear.

In one corner of the waiting room a TV is suspended, its volume so low that the newscaster seems to be mumbling. T.J. wants to yell, "Speak up!" like one foster mother used to yell at him. She was about ninety years old.

He glances toward the receptionist behind the counter, then gets up off his chair, clutching the large book he brought from the house awkwardly under his arm, and approaches the woman. Her perfume envelops him, reminding him, for one breath, of his real mother. A paper turkey is tacked to a bulletin board on a partition behind the counter. T.J. counts to thirty-seven before the receptionist looks up.

"May I help you?" she asks, squinting at him as if to assess any illness or injury that might have brought him to the ER.

"I just wondered. Could you please tell me what time it is?"

She frowns and looks at her watch. "Eleven forty-eight."

"Thank you."

He half expects her to say, "You're a polite young man!" He smiles at the woman, but she has already bent back over the computer keyboard. He remembers being called polite by one set of parents after they'd met him and Angela at an adoption party—the kind of party where kids who are available for adoption are brought to meet parents who are looking for kids. After saying T.J. was polite, the woman, the possible mother, went on, "And the little girl is so petite and absolutely adorable. But we can't adopt *two*."

Their social worker, Mrs. Cox, realized that T.J. was listening. She shushed the woman and her husband and whisked them away to have some red punch that tasted like medicine. He never saw them again.

T.J. goes back to his chair and sits.

Wait, *wait* ... Wait, *wait* ... The word has become a heartbeat.

A dull pain begins gnawing inside his belly. The pain is familiar. Something bad is happening, somewhere beyond his vision. Like the time their real mother came home with stitches on her face. Or the time he couldn't find his soft gray kitten after Momma put her outside for some "fresh air." The kitten never came back.

T.J. stares at the cover of the book in his lap. It's not really a book. It's a photo album with the words *My Life Book* neatly stenciled across the front. His sweaty fingers are sticking to the cover.

After Angela fell and Dan saw her lying there and Marlene called 911, it didn't take long for the EMTs to arrive and for Dan to ask questions and start giving orders. "We're going to the hospital. We'll follow the ambulance. Let's get going! Now!"

While Angela was being carried out of the house, Dan was yelling at Marlene to get the car keys and telling T.J., "Bring a book! It'll be a long wait."

Wait for what? T.J. asked himself. He had watched the EMTs working on his sister. She looked dead already. She wasn't twisted or broken, but she didn't move at all. And she wasn't sucking her thumb.

Dead, he thought, like the pigeon they'd found lying on the pavement outside the apartment where they were living with Momma. They had just gotten off the school bus. Angela had been little then. Probably only four. No, five, because she'd been in kindergarten. She'd shoved at the dead bird with the toe of her sneaker. "What's wrong with it?" she'd asked him. And he'd told her. Now she was as still as that grounded bird.

The alive Angela was never still, not even in her sleep. He could remember her kicking him over and over with her small, hard heels on the foldout couch they shared when they lived with their real mother. The kicks hurt, and he'd give her a shove or a sharp jab with his fist to get her to quit.

"Hurry, Timothy!" Marlene's voice was as tight as a rubber band stretched to the breaking point.

He didn't want to go to the Emergency Room.

But in that house there wasn't any choice. You were part of the family. You did certain things because that's just what families did. You were supposed to do what your mother or father told you to do.

Read a book! That was one of Dan's favorite phrases. Dan, the man with a computer job, who acted and talked like a teacher. "Timothy, why don't you just go read a book instead of moping around the house?" he'd say. "Turn off the TV and read, for heaven's sake." Or, at supper, "What've you been reading lately, Timothy?"

But T.J., who loved books when he was little, is not much of a reader now. He knows this annoys Dan, and sometimes what he wants to do most in the world is annoy Dan. So when Dan told him to bring a book to the ER, he deliberately picked a book that didn't need to be read—a book he knows by heart.

2

As a distraction, to keep from looking at the other people who're waiting, T.J. opens the photo album. His own face is reflected in the plastic covering on the first page. For a moment T.J. stares at himself—a narrow face, dark hair, and even darker eyes.

Then, with an effort, he focuses on the picture *beneath* the reflection. It's a 5 x 7 color photo of a smiling woman with lots of red-gold hair hanging around her face. One corner of the picture is creased, and there is a smudge that nearly obscures one of Momma's blue eyes.

BETWEEN THEN AND NOW—

"We're going to make life books," said Mrs. Cox, who was their own special caseworker. This was over a year ago, shortly after school started. In just three weeks they'd be moving out of foster care—forever, Mrs. Cox insisted—into an adoptive home. T.J. knew that Angela didn't understand what that meant. She was only seven at the time, but he was eleven, and understood.

He did not want to make a life book.

Mrs. Cox had insisted that he collect every photo, every paper keepsake he owned. He'd grudgingly gone through the small cardboard box of special stuff that he kept under his bed in the foster home where he and Angela were living. The box smelled musty. There wasn't much in it. And Angela, being so much younger, had even less—just her collection of paper birds.

"Is this the only photo you have of your birth mother?" Mrs. Cox asked, as if she didn't think that was possible. "If it is, I'll make a copy, so Angela can have one for her life book, too."

T.J. didn't bother to answer. As usual, Mrs. Cox just kept talking. "I know you think making a life book is a silly idea, T.J., but it helps to straighten out the memories. And gives you something special to take with you when you go to your new, adoptive home. In all my years of working with children just like you, I've found it to be a valuable experience."

He wondered how many children she'd worked with who were just like him. He imagined a whole roomful of T.J.s lined up one behind the other.

He'd been putting glue on the back of the picture of Momma. Lots of it. He didn't want to think about an adoptive home. Different from a foster home, this new home with parents called Marlene and Dan Westel. He and Angela had met these people. They were okay. They wore nice clothes and had amazingly white teeth that showed when they talked and smiled.

"Wait, T.J.! You don't need any glue," Mrs. Cox said loudly. "See, this photo album already has sticky stuff on each page. I brought the glue just in case you wanted to make a collage or something." She wrinkled her nose at the glue that dripped off the back of the photo and onto the Formica top of the large table. "Well ..." He could tell she was giving up. "I can't make a copy of it now. It would get glue all over the copier. I guess Angela doesn't have to have a picture of your birth mother. You can share yours with her whenever she wants to see it."

T.J. licked glue off his fingers, expecting Mrs. Cox to object, but she didn't seem to notice.

Angela was sitting at the same table in the small conference room at the Agency for Family and Children's Services building. But she hadn't even opened the pink photo album that Mrs. Cox had brought for her. Angela was folding a piece of paper into a shape. A bird shape.

T.J. remembered that it was Ray who taught Angela how to take a plain piece of paper and fold it this way and that until it became a tiny bird. Ray said these birds were called cranes. Even though T.J. was lots older than Angela—almost exactly four years—he hadn't been able to get the birds to turn out. His attempts had become lumps of twisted paper. But Ray didn't mind.

Ray was the man who T.J. wished had married Momma. But T.J. didn't want to think about that now.

Angela had become obsessed with making these paper birds. Most of them she kept in a huge tin can that had once contained three different flavors of popcorn. The can had a picture of kittens who were playing with yarn that was twined all around the can in interesting designs. That can of popcorn had been a Christmas present from Momma when they'd stayed with the people in the blue house. Their first foster home. T.J. thought it was amazing. Somehow that can had still been around later, when Angela began making her paper birds.

What had that blue-house foster family's last name been? He couldn't remember. Not their name. Not the names of the other kids who'd lived there. But one of the cats had been called Felicity Feline. He liked that name, and the cat had been gray, just like his kitten. But now, thinking back, he wasn't sure which had come first, the cat at the foster home or the kitten with his real mother.

Mrs. Cox moved over toward Angela. "Honey, how about we draw a picture of your birth mother? Or would you like to make a picture of the first house you remember living in, or maybe draw a portrait of your favorite foster brother or sister?"

Even T.J. knew Mrs. Cox was offering way too many choices for a seven-year-old. He knew how to get Angela to cooperate. He could play their "pretty please" game. This involved him basically pretending to beg her to do something by saying "Pretty please with ..." and adding treats like sugar, chocolate sauce, strawberries. Angela would get hooked, listening to the list of goodies "on top," until he'd say, "Coconut!" and she'd giggle and reply, "I hate coconut!" But by then she was usually willing to go along with the original request.

Right now, though, T.J. was not in the mood for games of any kind.

Angela glanced up from the purple paper bird that she had almost finished. "I'm going to fly this one off the roof," she said.

"No, I don't think so," Mrs. Cox said quickly. "Not the roof. That's too high, Angela."

"We should go up there," said Angela. "And inspectigate."

"What?" asked Mrs. Cox.

"She's talking in Angelese," said T.J. "That's what we call it. She uses big words wrong or makes up new words sometimes. Like combinations? 'Inspect' and 'investigate' make 'inspectigate.'"

Mrs. Cox nodded as she began moving some paper and crayons around on the table, in what she must have thought was an enticing manner. Angela continued to work on the tiny bird.

"Well ..." Mrs. Cox said with a sigh. "That's lovely, Angela. I should get a book on origami and teach you how to make some other animals."

T.J. knew that Angela could already make other folded animals. She was good at drawing, too. She could draw better at seven than he could at eleven. But he wasn't surprised when she said to Mrs. Cox, "No. I only like to make cranes. They can fly."

"Yes, there's always that." Mrs. Cox sounded tired.

On the car ride from their foster home to the AFCS building, Angela had taken three wrinkled paper birds out of her pocket and opened the window and tossed them out. Mrs. Cox scolded her for littering, but Angela said stubbornly that she was letting her birds go free and that they were flying away. She didn't seem aware that the stupid paper cranes had been swept backwards in the air for only a moment and then had crash-landed on the street. Nothing but tiny scraps of colored trash.

T.J. put the photo of their birth mother in the middle of the first page of his life book. The glue on the back made it slip, and when he let the plastic covering drop back in place over it, the glue squeezed out all around the edges and made a halo of white.

"You could write some information to put under the picture," Mrs. Cox said. "I brought all sorts of colored paper and lots of markers. You know, you could write your mother's name and maybe some of the things … the stories … she used to tell you when you were little. Or whatever you'd like, T.J."

There was certainly plenty of room. The picture filled only the middle of the page, and it had slid so that it wasn't centered and was crooked. He told himself that he didn't care.

"Your mother looks beautiful in that picture," Mrs. Cox said. "After you're done with this project, maybe you could write a letter to your birth mother? Tell her what you're putting in your life book."

T.J. stared at Mrs. Cox. Hard. Angela stopped folding and pressing a second piece of paper. She stuck her thumb in her mouth and looked at Mrs. Cox.

"Why would I do that?" he asked.

The frozen smile on Mrs. Cox's face suddenly cracked. Her lips twitched. "I'm sorry, T.J. I forgot for a moment that you don't—"

"Our momma's dead," Angela interrupted.

Before Mrs. Cox could start up where she'd left off, T.J. said, "So why would I write her a dumb letter about my stupid life book?"

NOW—

But as he sits in the waiting room, a letter writes itself inside his head.

Dear Momma,

Here's a picture of you when we were happy. Do you remember those days?

Can dead people remember?

    Your son,

    T. J.

3

"Timothy?"

He slams his life book shut and looks up into Marlene's face. She's standing directly in front of him, but he didn't see or hear her coming.

"I'm sorry you've been waiting here alone. But I ... your dad ... the doctors don't think you should come back there." Marlene stays standing, her arms bent as if inviting a comforting hug.

T.J. waits. He doesn't ask about Angela. His fingers feel stiff and moist where they are touching the cover of his life book.

"She's still not awake," Marlene says quietly. "They're doing tests. X-rays and all that. Only more complicated. A CAT scan. You know."

T.J. says nothing.

"Are you okay? Do you need anything? Here. Here's some money." She dumps a pile of change into his cupped hand.

The coins are cool on his warm palm. "Go get yourself some juice, apple or orange, plus something to eat. There are machines around that corner." Marlene points and T.J. turns his head to look. But his stomach is clenched around that familiar pain, holding it tightly inside him. No way can he eat anything.

Marlene reaches out to brush a strand of hair off his forehead, and he ducks instinctively. She draws back, frowning, then says, "I'll come for you as soon as they say you can see her. But right now—it's not a good time."

T.J. tries to look into his adoptive mother's eyes, but she is already turning toward the swinging doors.

She calls back to him, "Be sure to get some food, Timothy. It's time for lunch, but we can't leave Angela. We don't want you getting sick from not eating."

T.J. is silent. He feels a tiny measure of relief, like when you open the refrigerator door on a really hot day and you breathe in a little blast of chilled air. Marlene didn't say that Angela was dead. And she didn't mention anything about Angela's fall. Or why it happened. Not yet.

His mouth feels dry. He thinks about his tongue, wondering if it'll stick to his teeth if he doesn't get a drink soon. He's not thinking about Angela behind those doors, having weird stuff—tests—done to her.

He stands up and dumps all the change Marlene gave him into the left front pocket of his jeans. It feels heavy. Then he sits down again and carefully pries open his life book to the second page.

BETWEEN THEN AND NOW—

"Draw a picture of the first house you remember, T.J. It can be one you lived in with your birth mother or a foster home. Put in lots of details." Mrs. Cox was sounding helpful and supportive. It was her job.

T.J. grabbed the top piece of construction paper off the neat pile Mrs. Cox had arranged on the table halfway between him and his sister. The paper was brown. He used a black magic marker to draw a rectangle with a triangle for the roof. Next he selected a blue marker and began coloring in the house. The blue on top of brown turned a dark, nondescript color, almost black. The picture looked like something a baby would draw. Not worthy of an eleven-year-old. He pretended he didn't care.

Mrs. Cox was busy trying to get Angela to do something—anything—other than make yet another folded bird.

T.J. had really wanted to draw that blue house, but it looked all wrong. He thought about crumpling up the stupid picture and tossing it onto the floor. If he did, Mrs. Cox would insist that he get up and take it over to the wastebasket by the door, so instead he began drawing a tree next to the house. He tried to make a cat, balancing on one limb. Felicity Feline. He wrote her name in the space above the stick-figure cat, but the marker was too thick, so the letters got all mushed together. And he wasn't exactly sure how to spell Felicity.

Spelling was not his favorite subject. Funny how reading could be so easy but spelling so hard. Actually, nothing about school was a favorite with T.J. Maybe recess if nobody was picking on him or Angela.

"You lived in a black house?" Mrs. Cox sounded concerned.

T.J. shook his head and said, "It's supposed to be blue."

"Oh, well, here, why don't you start over? Use this white paper. That way the blue will turn out blue. Or better yet, use crayons. When you're filling in a large area, crayons work better than markers. Don't you think?"

"No," said T.J.

Mrs. Cox sighed. "Maybe we've done enough for one session. Neither of you seems to be trying. I mean, these books are something you can treasure the rest of your lives. You can show them to your new family. Marlene is a scrapbooker herself. She will love looking at your life books! You can add on new pages after you move in with Dan and Marlene. And

I'm certain they will be interested in your past. In everything about you."

He didn't believe Mrs. Cox. There were a lot of things T.J. didn't think his new parents would want to know. There were things he didn't want to remember himself.

Mrs. Cox glanced at her watch and sighed again. Evidently it wasn't yet time to take them back to their foster home.

"Here." Mrs. Cox handed him an unlined 3 x 5 card. "Write down your memories about this house, T.J. You don't have to draw it over if you don't want to."

He sat for a few minutes with a thin magic marker in his hand. He was aware of Angela humming softly to herself as she folded an orange bird. She had finished a pink bird, too, and set it on the table next to the purple one. The paper cranes looked as if they'd fallen, each listing to a side on bent wingtips.

T.J. wrote carefully. *This was are house for a wile. I licked living there. They had a lot of cats. I don't rememmber there names. I mean the peple. The cats had good names like Felcity Felin.*

He stuck the card under the drab picture of the house. He wished that Mrs. Cox had insisted that he redo the drawing, but he didn't want her to think he agreed with her about how lousy it looked, so he left it alone.

NOW—

T.J. stares at the picture in his life book and then shuts his eyes, trying to remember that blue house the way it really looked. But he imagines it just like his babyish drawing— crooked, smudged. Best forgotten.

But he can't forget the days leading up to their going there.

It all started when Momma left them with her friend Tanya. He was little then, years younger than Angela is now. He had just started kindergarten, and Angela was toddling around, wearing diapers that gave her a fat butt and smelled worse than dog poop.

4

"Celia, not again!" Tanya said to Momma.

Momma smiled as if she couldn't tell that her friend was angry. But T.J. knew, even though he was only five, that Tanya was trying not to blow up in front of him and Angela.

"It's only for a couple of hours, Tanya! For God's sake, I need a break. I'm just going to get my hair done. I'll pay you this time. I promise."

"Sure. You bet." Tanya picked up Angela, who smiled sweetly and patted Tanya's plump bare arm. "Okay, whatever. But listen, Celia, next time call me before you come over to drop off your kids. I'm not always home! And I've got a job interview I can't afford to miss. I mean it! You'd better be back to get these kids real soon. You hear me?"

"Don't worry! I'll be back. Couple of hours is all!"

T.J. watched Momma leave, swinging her hips and her purse as she went down the front walk. Her reddish hair looked alive, almost like flames, licking at her shoulders. He knew she wasn't getting her hair done. She'd met a new man. He'd heard her talking to him on the phone. The man had wanted to come over to visit at their apartment, but she said no, she wanted to have fun someplace else, and she arranged to meet him at a bar.

"It's okay, kiddos," Tanya reassured them after their mother hopped into her little rusty car and roared off. "My job interview isn't until tomorrow morning. Your momma will be back way before then."

But she didn't come back for them. Not that night. Not the next morning. Tanya's hands as she scrubbed his face with a smelly washcloth were rough like anger. "I am not happy with your mother," she whispered to him so Angela wouldn't hear and wake up. Tanya's breath smelled like something dead. "Where is your mother? I've called your apartment five times. No answer. Not even a machine. And all I get on her cell phone is some crappy music. I've left three messages, but do you think she gets back to me?"

Tanya cursed when she heard Angela beginning to whimper on the couch.

T.J.'s stomach hurt. He decided he didn't much like Tanya. She was messy, even when she was supposed to be getting ready for a job interview. Momma could get tired-looking, but when she got ready to go out—anywhere—she always looked good. She'd brush her shiny hair and put on blush and lipstick and suddenly she was beautiful. And the men would notice her. She had a way of walking that made T.J. feel proud and uneasy, all mixed up together. Men would yell things at her, things he didn't understand. She'd laugh and toss her hair. Sometimes she'd yell back at them, depending on her mood.

Momma had moods. That morning, with Tanya cursing and running around her house trying to figure out what to wear for the job interview, he guessed that his mother just hadn't been in the mood to come pick them up.

"I don't know what to do," Tanya said, coming back from her bedroom wearing a skirt that looked way too long in the back and too short in the front.

"You can leave us here," T.J. said slowly. "We'll be okay. I can look after Angela. She's good in the morning. She likes to watch cartoons."

Tanya looked at him sharply. "Does your momma sometimes … I mean—do you watch Angela sometimes? All by yourself?"

Later, he wished he'd lied. He wished he'd said, "No! Never!" But he was scared that Tanya would get even madder at his mother. He didn't like people to be angry with Momma because sometimes they did bad things to her or even to him and Angela. He had some vivid memories of being hit by men whose faces were indistinct blurs. So that morning, he told the truth. "Yeah. She leaves me in charge. I'm good at watching Angela. Except for changing her. Could you change her diaper?"

"I haven't got any more diapers! Your mother only gave me one. 'Couple of hours.' Remember? That's how long she said she'd be gone. Oh, God, I'm going to be late!"

"We'll be okay," he said.

Finally, muttering and yanking at the hem of her skirt, Tanya left.

In the bottom food cupboard T.J. found some cereal. He got a bowl of it ready for Angela, but she wasn't hungry. When she spilled all the milk down her shirt and began to cry, he got mad and slapped her hand the way Momma always did. He helped her down off the chair, but she slipped on a puddle of milk and fell and cried harder. He could tell she needed to be changed, and it wasn't just pee in her diaper. Yesterday, Momma had been cursing about how Angela had diaper rash again. So now his little sister was dirty and hurting. Was that why she wouldn't quit crying?

When he yelled at her, Angela sobbed harder. He decided to take off the dirty diaper and try to clean her up. But when he did that, poop got all over his hands, and while he was washing off in the bathroom sink, Angela sat her dirty butt down on the rug in the living room. The rug must have been prickly, because she cried louder and louder. Suddenly she was banging her feet and fists on the floor, having a tantrum.

And then he heard some other banging. Someone was at the door. He was sure it was Momma. He was so happy to run to the door and unlock it and swing it open.

But it was a stranger standing there, an older woman with glasses and a pinched-up mouth.

"Are you children *alone*?" she asked, peering into Tanya's living room.

Alone? T.J. started to say that Angela was with *him*, so neither of them was alone. But he soon realized that the woman meant no grownup was with them. He didn't know that being left alone was such a big deal.

But the woman thought it was, and she insisted on coming in, though he tried to tell her that this was Tanya's place and she might be mad at him for letting in a stranger. Even if it was a neighbor, as this person claimed to be.

Then the woman used Tanya's phone, which he didn't like either. And she gave Angela a bath. Angela loved it and played and laughed in the soap bubbles and made him feel as if he was a terrible big brother because all she did for *him* was cry and cry.

And then, next thing he knew, although this memory wasn't very clear, there were a couple of police officers standing in Tanya's living room, and then Tanya was home and crying almost as hard as Angela had been before the neighbor showed up. By this time T.J.'s head was hurting from all the confusion.

Tanya stopped crying and started saying all sorts of stuff about their momma. How she'd leave the kids with her, sometimes for days, without even saying when she'd be back. And how the little boy, T.J., had told her that their mother left him alone with the baby.

Angela's not really a baby, he wanted to say. *She can walk.* But his mouth felt glued shut.

"It's like Celia just disappears off the face of the earth," Tanya told the policemen standing in her apartment.

He and Angela got a ride in a police car that time. And they ended up with the people in the blue house. They lived there for what seemed like a long time. Maybe a year. Felicity Feline had been the best part of that foster home. Funny how he couldn't remember the parents' names at all.

NOW—

T.J. looks up from his life book.

Some new people have come into the ER waiting room, and the baby with its teenage mother has been called through the swinging doors. He glances back down at the photo album. With one finger he traces the outline of the blue house as he imagines writing another letter.

Dear Momma,

The blue house people were okay. But we wanted to stay with you.

So, where did you and that guy go that was so much fun? You forgot all about me and Angela. Were you surprised when you came back to Tanya's house and we weren't there?

I remember how mad you were later when we went back to live with you. You said it was all that stupid Tanya's fault for leaving us by ourselves in her dirty house. You said she should have known better.

It was nice to have you mad at someone else. For a change.

    Your son,
    T.J. (Not Timothy)

He closes his eyes and listens, as if expecting Momma to reply. Instead he hears someone coughing, more like gagging. T.J. wants to leave the waiting room so badly his feet itch. He holds his breath, hoping that those coughed-up germs will settle and he won't inhale them. He manages to count to twenty-four, takes a breath, and turns to the next page.

5

Party Time is printed in capital letters on a piece of red paper above the next sloppy picture in his life book. By page three, Mrs. Cox gave up trying to encourage his artistic skills.

The party had been Momma's idea, a surprise for him and Angela when they came back from the blue house.

T.J. used every single one of Mrs. Cox's colored markers to draw the streamers Momma had hung above the table. In his picture it's hard to see the three people—Momma, Angela, and himself—drawn in brown beneath all those colorful streamers.

THEN—

It was the best party T.J. could remember having in his whole life. Momma was so happy, with a smile that was brighter than any magic marker could make it look. She was wearing lipstick called Moonstruck Pink. He knew the name because sometimes Momma dumped all her stuff out of her purse when she was looking for things. Like her car keys. There was no magic marker color that could match Moonstruck Pink, so he used red when he drew it later.

Momma had bought a cake for the party. The frosting was white, but on top of the cake were pink, yellow, and purple flowers and the words *Welcome Home* written in green frosting to match the leaves on the flowers. Angela was way too little to read, but T.J. sounded out the words, and Momma was so proud of him.

"Right! Welcome home!" she said with a big smile. "You are such a good reader, T.J.!"

T.J. felt a warm rush so intense that he almost jumped down off his chair and ran over to hug his mother. But Angela, sitting across from him, was banging her spoon on the table. Then she took her thumb out of her mouth and chanted, "Cake! Cake! Cake!"

Momma cut the cake and served it with peppermint ice cream. T.J.'s tongue always felt tingly when he ate that flavor, but he didn't mind.

"This is the way it should be," Momma said as they stuffed cake and ice cream into their mouths. "Just the three of us. No stupid Tanya around, messing up our lives."

"No more 'Tupid Tanya!" cried Angela, and Momma laughed so hard she started to cough.

They had leftover cake and ice cream for supper that night.

T.J. thought it was the most delicious cake he'd ever tasted. Way sweeter than that cake the blue-house foster mother had baked for him on his last birthday, when he'd turned six. That pretend mother had been surprised because he hadn't known about making a wish before blowing out the candles. Momma always said birthdays were way overrated, so why have cake?

While T.J. and Angela were in foster care, Momma had gotten a job, so now a neighbor lady came in to watch Angela each weekday. She arrived a little before Momma left for work and before T.J. went to school, and she was still there when he came home.

Her name was Betty, and she had fingernails that were so long T.J. was afraid she would scratch or spear him when she helped him off with his coat. Betty painted her nails dark red, like blood. T.J. started taking his coat and hat off in the hallway, before even getting to their apartment door.

Once in a while another lady came to talk to them. Momma said she was a social worker, and T.J. was suspicious because he'd met social workers when he and Angela lived in the blue house. But Momma said, "You are such a worrier, T.J. I bet your initials stand for Too Jumpy."

"No, they don't," he said.

"Oh, really? I'm sorry. You're not Too Jumpy?" Momma giggled and reached out to tickle T.J.'s tummy. He laughed and jumped out of her reach.

"See? You *are* too jumpy! You're my big jumpy boy. A first grader! Remember, everything is fine. I have a job, and Betty comes every day. No more worrying, T.J."

Betty told him and Angela that she had an adorable, precious toy poodle at home. She called it a "teacup poodle," and when he asked why, she said she'd show him. So one day she brought the toy poodle along, but it wasn't a toy at all. It was a live dog that skittered around the apartment barking nonstop in such a high pitch that Angela covered her ears.

By the time T.J. got home from school that day, the dog had made a couple of puddles on the rug that were bigger than the dog. Betty showed him and Angela how the tiny black bit of living fluff could fit into a cup on the table. T.J. liked the way the dog licked his fingers with its little pink tongue.

Later, when Momma got home, T.J. said, "Betty put a cup on the table and her dog fit inside it."

"Right on the *table?*" Momma rolled her eyes. "Batty Betty," she muttered. "I may have to throw away that cup."

From then on, Momma always called their babysitter by that name, so it was no wonder Angela started saying it too.

—

During summer vacation, when T.J. was home with Angela and Betty, they spent most of the time watching TV. Angela was bored and tried to get Betty's attention by acting up. She would strip off her clothes and race naked around the living room, giggling. Betty was horrified. She spent a lot of each day chasing Angela and struggling to get her T-shirt and jeans back on.

Sometimes Angela would dance in front of the TV screen, singing at the top of her lungs. Betty would shake her head and say, "Please give me some peace and quiet!" Then she'd resort to swatting at Angela's bottom as she sashayed past the couch.

Angela began to hide from Betty by scooting under the kitchen table. When Betty yelled at her, Angela yelled back, "I want a piece of quiet!"

T.J. liked that phrase, "a piece of quiet," and tried to imagine what it would be like to have a piece of quiet. He pictured it being pale blue with swirls of mint green.

One day, near the end of that summer, after Betty had been coming so long that T.J. was beginning to feel comfortable with her, Angela called her Batty Betty to her face, and added, "I deafeningly hate you!"

Soon after that, Betty told Momma she had better things to do than watch a spoiled kid all day. "I've stood it long enough. I quit! The boy is okay, but you're going to have your hands full with that little girl. Just turned three, and what a mouth. Mark my words!"

T.J. didn't think Angela was so bad—not nearly as mouthy as some of the kids at school, anyway. He was starting second grade and heard lots of swearing and screaming on the playground and sometimes in the classroom. Maybe Betty just didn't like kids as much as she liked teacup poodles.

With no Batty Betty around, Momma stopped going to work, which suited her fine, she said, because that job insulted her intelligence, waiting on idiots all day.

But Momma wasn't happy being at home. Kids got on her nerves, and she needed time alone, and how was she ever going to have any free time with two kids, for God's sake? T.J. wanted to point out that he was gone all day, at school. But he decided being quiet might be the best reaction. When Momma talked like that, T.J. felt a knot in his throat. If he swallowed too hard, that pain would start in his belly.

Angela always managed to have a tantrum shortly after all that complaining about kids, as if she wanted to make sure Momma had a good reason to hate being home.

Momma wanted to get out. She wanted to go have some fun. T.J. thought he understood. Momma was like the fragile green bug with transparent wings that had wandered into the living room one night. It had circled the lamp next to the couch where he and Angela were supposed to be sleeping. The little bug tried to get closer and closer to the light, which T.J. finally turned off, despite Angela's squeals of protest, just so he wouldn't hear the incessant *ping, ping, ping* of the bug hitting the bulb. In the morning, the insect was gone. Nightlife—bars and men and music—were like a lamp to Momma, drawing her away from home when night came.

But when Betty had announced she was quitting, Momma had given her a piece of her mind, so now she couldn't ask Betty to babysit evenings. And there didn't seem to be anyone else to do it.

Finally Momma began going out when he and Angela were in bed for the night. Only he was hardly ever asleep. He worried about some nosy neighbor calling the police to report on two kids being alone.

One night he heard a knock on their door, and he huddled under his blanket, his heart leaping with fear. Then he realized that it was Momma's voice, yelling in the hallway. She'd forgotten her key. She thanked him with a big hug and kiss when he let her inside.

Momma was trying to quit smoking, but she smelled like cigarettes and beer. He decided he didn't mind.

For Christmas that year, when T.J. was in second grade, Momma bought a huge TV, a dinette set, and a new convertible couch. "We need something to make life worth living," she explained. "I don't even have to make any payments till the new year."

"It feels like my teddy bear, Momma," said Angela, running her fingers along the back of the couch. "It's so pretty! It's george's!"

Momma laughed. "You mean *gorgeous*."

T.J. grinned and said, "She's talking in Angela language."

He was pleased when Momma smiled and said, "She speaks Angelese," and gave them both hugs.

Later, when the bills started piling up, Momma borrowed from a place on Baker Street. But she told T.J. that she had no money to keep up payments to the "loan sharks," as she called them.

Even though T.J. knew she wasn't talking about real sharks, he pictured huge greenish gray ones, crawling on their fins, opening their jaws to snap at Momma's high heels as she stumbled down the street. Then these shark people began calling nearly every day. Momma refused to answer the phone in the kitchen, and she kept her cell phone turned off. But sometimes T.J. picked up the house phone because he couldn't stand the constant ringing. People with rough, scaly voices left their numbers. He could imagine their sharp teeth clicking. But Momma never, ever called them back. The calls stopped when the phone got disconnected because she didn't pay the bill.

Next Momma borrowed money to pay back the loan. She got the money from a man she met at the bar, Pete's Place, right around the corner from their apartment. This man understood about debts, Momma told T.J., and now their troubles were over. But the man, whose name T.J. couldn't remember (or maybe he had never known it), began showing up every time the welfare check came. And even when Momma cried and begged, the man didn't act understanding at all. He would wave his arms and shout, and his beer belly bounced. T.J. began thinking of him as B.B., for Beer Belly.

B.B. always tried to get Momma to talk to him in her bedroom, but Momma said that the living room was the place to conduct business. Sometimes he brought gifts for T.J. and Angela, who was too little to act cool about these things. She always giggled and starting playing with the present—a paddleball or a coloring book and some crayons.

T.J. knew better. He always said, "No thanks," when the gift was offered. But then B.B. would turn around and give whatever had been meant for T.J. to Angela. He must have known that later T.J. would play with the water pistol or plastic dinosaurs.

After B.B. and Momma's business was done—the handing over of an envelope of money—B.B. always wanted to stay, but Momma insisted that he leave. She came up with excuses. She usually said her boyfriend was coming over. T.J. knew there was no boyfriend then, but he kept quiet.

Before B.B. left, he always grabbed Momma and kissed her right on the lips. After the door was closed, Momma would run to the sink and spit and wash out her mouth. She seemed to think those kisses were as bad as losing their money.

Hours after B.B.'s visits, T.J. could still smell cigarettes and sweat, as if a part of the guy had stayed behind, lurking in the air, watching them and waiting.

Momma said, "That man gives me the creeps!" And T.J. nodded.

6

"There's only one solution," Momma announced on a Friday afternoon when T.J. got home from school. His jacket was damp from the spring rain that had been spitting from a dirty-looking sky all day. "Since I can't find a job to fit my skills, we're going to your grandma's house."

T.J. frowned. He didn't remember a grandmother at all. But Momma talked on and on in a bright, false voice about how he *must* remember his grandmother and grandfather.

A grandfather too, thought T.J. uneasily. All day Saturday, while the rain tapped against the windows, Momma packed their things in plastic garbage bags, labeled with strips of masking tape: *T.J.'s clothes. Toys and Junk. Angela's clothes.*

On Sunday morning the sun came out, and Momma said, "We're leaving."

She was dressed funny that day. Instead of her usual pretty shirt and tight pants, she was wearing a pair of baggy slacks and a white shirt with a collar and a necklace T.J. had never seen before.

"That's so pretty," said Angela, reaching up to pat the necklace.

Momma said, "Yeah, well, my mother gave it to me, and I thought I'd wear it today." She sounded distracted, and T.J. was surprised to see a huge stack of bulging boxes that she had packed during the night. It looked as if she was clearing out the place.

"Are we moving?" he asked, confused.

"Let's hope so," said Momma, smiling, but her brow puckered as she glanced in the mirror.

"You look beautiful," he told her. And this time her smile was real.

Momma forced Angela into diapers that morning even though she'd gotten toilet-trained way back when they lived in the blue house.

"With diapers on, you can pee to your heart's content," Momma told her, "and we won't have to be stopping every five miles at some cruddy gas station."

Angela yelled, "I'm three and a half! I don't wear diapers. I'm a big girl now!"

Momma tried ignoring her at first, but Angela fussed and fumed until Momma yelled at her so loudly that T.J.'s head began to ache.

While Angela sulked in the bathroom, T.J. helped Momma carry armloads of their belongings to the car. "We'll come back later for the rest of the boxes," Momma said when they couldn't squeeze in anything else. T.J. kept his mouth shut and didn't ask about the furniture they were leaving behind.

Momma sent him to get Angela. "Get outta my privacy!" she yelled when he knocked on the bathroom door.

"Please come out."

No answer.

"Pretty please with a cherry on top?"

No answer.

"Pretty please with a cherry, and sugar, and honey, and whipped cream, and coconut ..."

The door opened. Angela stepped out and said, "No coconut! You *know* I hate coconut." But she had the trace of a grin on her face.

He had to sit in back to "keep Angela entertained," Momma said. And the front seat was piled nearly to the roof with boxes anyway.

They stopped to fill up with gas at the corner station, so an hour later, when the car sputtered and lurched, she said, "We can't be out of gas! My God, we're only halfway there!" Then she cursed a lot as she pulled onto the gravel shoulder of the road. T.J.'s stomach tightened, and he pushed the button, opening his window a moment before the engine died.

Momma tried to restart the car, but each time she turned the key there was a harsh, grinding noise, so she gave up and got out. Traffic was whipping past, and T.J. saw Momma's hair lifted by the air currents and tossed over her face. She pounded on the hood of the car and came back to peer in at the two children with tears in her eyes.

"I can't believe this is happening! This damn car has run for … what? Three years, isn't it? And now, *now*, it decides to quit. I hate my life!"

"Momma, don't worry," T.J. said in a small voice. He didn't like her to say she hated her life. He and Angela were part of her life. But Momma's bright eyes swept right over him as if she had been talking to the air, not to him or his sister.

"What am I going to do?" Momma asked the air, and T.J. wished he were a grownup with answers instead of a seven-and-a-half-year-old kid. She glanced up and down the road, but traffic kept swooshing past as if this were a race. And their car had been disqualified.

T.J. looked at Angela. She was sucking her thumb, and her blue eyes were filmed with tears. He hoped she wouldn't have a tantrum. That was the last thing—the very last thing—they needed.

"I could walk to a gas station or somebody's house." Momma had climbed back into the car and sat slumped in the driver's seat. "But I don't dare leave you two here *alone*, right?" she said sarcastically. "If only I hadn't lost my cell phone …" Momma seemed close to tears again. More sad now than angry.

"Somebody will help us," T.J. said.

"Yeah, right." Momma sounded so discouraged that Angela leaned forward and tried to pat their mother's shoulder. She couldn't reach it, of course, but the gesture made T.J. feel sorry for Angela too. His throat was getting tight.

Momma lit a cigarette while he and Angela sat as quiet as stones in the back seat. When she had finished and stubbed the butt out in the ashtray, Momma said, "Okay. I used to hitch when I was a teenager. Let's see if the old charms still work."

Suddenly she was sounding more like herself. He always had trouble keeping up with her moods. She acted almost happy as she reached into her purse and pulled out a brush and some makeup. In a few moments she stepped out of the car, looking as if she was ready to go out on the town.

T.J. counted the cars and trucks that went by. Only seven. Then a delivery truck of some sort pulled up behind them and a young man climbed out. "You having car trouble, miss?" he asked, jamming a baseball cap on his head. T.J. watched out the back window.

Momma walked toward him, tossing her hair out of her eyes expertly. "I am so embarrassed." Her voice was higher than usual. "I'm on my way to visit my folks, and this old thing"—she tapped the trunk of the car as she went past it—"just gave up the ghost."

"Well …" The guy had moved a little closer and was looking in the back window at T.J. He probably couldn't see Angela, since she was so short. But the expression on his face had changed. "I guess I could give you a lift. But I don't know that I'd have room for the kid."

"*Kids*," T.J. whispered to himself. Angela twisted next to him, trying to unfasten her seatbelt. "Don't do that!" he said to her.

She glared at him. "I wanna see too!"

"There's nothing to see. Just some guy who's going to help us."

"We gonna ride in his car?"

"No. Besides, he's got a truck."

"I gotta go potty," Angela said.

"Go in your pants, stupid. That's why you've got diapers on."

"I don't wanna," whimpered Angela.

The man was talking to Momma, and T.J. leaned close to the open window to hear. "If you want, you could call somebody with my phone," the man offered.

"That's awfully nice of you," Momma said. "But I don't think they'll be home. Not much point in calling somebody who's not home, right?"

T.J. wondered why their grandparents wouldn't be home. Then, abruptly, with a sick jolt in his stomach, he knew that Momma was lying. She didn't know whether they were home or not. She hadn't even told them about this visit.

The guy was looking uncomfortable. He'd just caught sight of Angela's blond head. She had unbuckled her seatbelt and was bouncing up and down, her hair tickling the side of T.J.'s face.

"I really got to get going," the truck driver said. "I'm sorry, but I don't have room. Not for *two* kids. You sure there's nobody you could call?"

"Okay. I'll call." Momma sounded sullen. She didn't even bother to brush back her hair as she followed the driver to the truck. He handed her a phone, and she stood right there, in front of the bumper of the truck, and called.

When she came back to the car, her mouth was set in a grim line.

"T.J.! Why couldn't you keep her hooked in? Why're you kids so nosy? God, I'd have gotten a ride to the doorstep if it weren't for you two!"

T.J. didn't answer. Usually Momma never even reminded them to buckle up. That was his responsibility. He'd given up trying to get Momma to wear her seatbelt. She said it hurt her belly or messed up her dress or her pants.

Momma climbed back into the car and slammed the door. She didn't wave as the truck pulled out around them with a cheery beep of its horn.

"Well, he's coming to pick us up," Momma said without expression.

"Who?" asked Angela.

"Who else? My father. Your grandfather."

Angela stuck one thumb in her mouth and with her other hand reached out for T.J. He found her palm sweaty and hot, but he tightened his fingers and squeezed gently.

7

THEN—

They waited a long time for their grandfather to arrive. Angela whined about going potty, but their mother said there was no way she was going to let her pee by the side of the road. "Go in your diapers, you silly baby," Momma said.

"I am absotively not a baby!" Angela began to sniffle, and Momma didn't joke about her speaking in Angelese.

Hearing all the talk about peeing made T.J. feel he had to go. But he held it.

Momma tried playing games with them to make the time pass, but Angela didn't know one license plate from another. When she got frustrated, she started crying and kicking the back of Momma's seat with her toes. Momma got mad. She twisted around, leaning through the opening between the front seats, and with the back of her hand she gave Angela a hard smack on the face.

T.J. watched the red mark appear and Angela's mouth twist into a strange, ugly shape as she cried harder. There wasn't much room for her to have a tantrum, but she slammed her feet everywhere and threw her head back and forth.

T.J. wished for a piece of quiet.

In the front seat Momma sat as still as one of the tree trunks along the side of the road. Finally Angela's sobs turned into little hiccups and then she fell asleep, slumped sideways with her neck bent. T.J. had nothing to say to his mother.

A large, dark car pulled up in the grass on the other side of the road, and when there was a break in the traffic, it made a U-turn and parked directly behind their disabled car. T.J. watched Momma's face in the rear-view mirror. Her brow was creased, and her lips were pressed tightly closed. But when T.J. heard the slam of the door to the other car, she nodded and said, "It's him."

Then she leaped out and ran back to meet a sandy-haired man dressed in jeans and a plaid shirt. He looked a lot younger than the grandfathers portrayed in books. The man opened his arms wide, and Momma, after a moment's hesitation, stepped toward him and returned his hug. Then the man came toward the car, leaning over slightly because he was so tall and wanted to see in the windows.

T.J. gave Angela a shove and she woke up, looking groggy and pink, wisps of hair clinging to her damp face. Her well-sucked thumb was wrinkled and wet.

"This is T.J.," Momma said. "And the one that's not quite awake, that's Angela."

"Good to meet you," Grandpa said as if he meant it. "Now you kids get out on the curb side so as not to be in front of some crazy driver. This road is one hell of a place to get stuck. You climb right in my car, and we'll get you home in no time."

"Did Mom come too?" asked Momma. Her voice sounded different, as if it had shriveled up. She glanced back at Grandpa's car and squinted.

"No, no. She's getting things ready. You know your mother. For the first few minutes after your call, she was … in shock, I guess you could say."

As Grandpa talked, T.J. and Angela scrambled out of the back seat and into the cavelike interior of Grandpa's car. It had a vaguely familiar odor, sort of like a new doll that

Angela had been given for Christmas at the blue house. A nice smell. Grandpa helped move all of their stuff. T.J. was surprised that most of the bags and boxes fit into the trunk. Finally, Grandpa climbed into the driver's seat, and Momma got in next to him, and they drove off to Grandma's.

Through T.J.'s head ran that old song they sang in school at Thanksgiving—or was it at Christmas?—about going to Grandmother's house. Now they were crossing over something that looked like a river and driving through some woods, but of course there was no horse. Or sleigh. And no snow.

Grandpa insisted on stopping to get them each a bottle of orange juice, and T.J. was glad to use the restroom. Angela seemed to have forgotten all about going potty. Probably she'd live in diapers the rest of her life, T.J. thought.

Their grandparents' house was in a town, and it had a fence and flowers blooming along the front walk. T.J. was reminded of a picture on a calendar he'd seen somewhere. The school office, maybe.

"Daffodils," said Momma, sounding almost happy. T.J. had been feeling sleepy, but now that they had arrived, he was wide awake and listening to the unfamiliar voice of his grandmother as she hurried off the front porch and toward the car.

"Celia! I can't believe you're here! It's been so long. Ten years, right?"

"I don't know, Mom. I haven't been counting. Obviously, you have." Momma sounded as if she was bored, suddenly. In the car, she'd been talking just fine to Grandpa.

T.J. stared at this new person who was his very own grandmother.

"Call me Grandma," she said pleasantly as he climbed out of the car.

Her hair was short and fluffy but the same shade of reddish gold as Momma's. Her face was freckled and rosy cheeked, and she was wearing glasses that had slid down her nose. Her jeans looked as if they'd just been washed, and her shirt was almost identical to the one Momma was wearing today.

Grandma pushed her glasses into place before she helped Angela out of the car and carried her up the sidewalk and right into the living room. T.J. followed. Then she set Angela down on the couch and gave him a warm, friendly hug. He liked her smell—powder and a perfume that made him think of summer.

"I'm making us some dinner. You kids must be famished. Both of you look way too thin."

T.J. could hear Momma and Grandpa talking as they carried some bags up onto the porch. But Grandma was keeping her voice down, as if she wanted to make sure only he and Angela heard her words. "We'll eat just as soon as you two freshen up and we get your belongings settled in your mother's old room. I am so glad to meet you. I had no idea … I mean, I knew about *you*, young man, but this little girl—not a word. Not *one* word."

Angela was looking lost, her hair tangled and mussed from the trip. On her face a reddish, angry mark showed where Momma had slapped her, and T.J. began sifting through excuses for its being there on Angela's perfect face. Grandma led them into the biggest kitchen T.J. had ever seen. The table was small, though, and covered with a brightly printed cloth. In the center of the table sat a bowl of apples, so shiny he decided they had to be fake.

"Have an apple if you'd like. That won't spoil your dinner," Grandma said.

T.J. shook his head quickly.

"What happened to your face, little one?" Grandma asked as she handed Angela a cup of milk. "You two sit right here and drink this milk while I help get things organized."

She left them alone together in the kitchen, and T.J. listened to her talking to Momma out in the living room. Somehow Grandma's voice sounded different when she asked Momma questions. Momma mumbled answers that he couldn't make out.

T.J. sipped the cold milk. It helped ease the tightness in his throat. Maybe the mark on Angela's face wasn't so bad. Grandma didn't seem to be that interested. But later, when she came back into the kitchen to check on the casserole in the oven, she asked about it again. Angela looked blank, as if she'd forgotten all about her tantrum and Momma's reaction.

So T.J. said, "She fell off her toy horse at home. It's not bad. But you should have heard her cry."

At dinner, Grandpa mentioned the slap mark, and before T.J. could say anything, Momma said, "Oh, these kids get in fights all the time. On the way here in the car, T.J. smacked her, but she deserved it."

Grandma looked sharply at T.J., and he had trouble swallowing the mouthful of noodles and meat in his mouth. "Well," was all she said. The expression on Grandma's face as she turned back toward his mother made him think maybe she already knew that Momma had trouble with the truth. And maybe that he did too.

That night, T.J. couldn't go to sleep. The big bed felt strange with Angela lying far on the other side. Momma was sleeping on the couch out in the living room. And Grandpa and Grandma were in their own room down the hall past the bathroom and another closed door. This house had no second floor, but Grandpa had shown him the basement that was semi-fixed up and even had a huge TV and a black leather reclining chair that looked big enough for him and Angela to sleep on.

As T.J. watched the numbers change on the luminous digital clock on the nightstand next to the bed, he thought he could live here for a long time.

Maybe here things would be okay.

8

The next morning, T.J. woke to find Angela no longer in the bed. Usually he was up way before her. This change, on top of all the others, made him feel anxious. He untangled his blanket, scrambled up, and dashed down the hallway to the bathroom, where he peed and splashed cold water on his face.

He'd gone to bed in his T-shirt and underwear, so now he went back into the bedroom, planning to get dressed in clean clothes. But the jumble of bags and boxes piled along the walls was daunting. He'd never find what he needed without digging for hours. So he put on the jeans and socks he'd worn the day before. They felt a little stiff and smelled like their city apartment.

His sneakers had disappeared. Maybe Grandma had put them away somewhere. He checked the small closet in the room. Mothball-scented dresses hung wadded together on a bar across the top, and the space on the floor was filled with neatly labeled boxes: *Christmas ornaments. Buttons. Old jewelry. Winter hats.* He saw no sneakers.

T.J. stepped back into the hallway and went to the closed door between their bedroom and the bathroom. It opened easily, but it didn't reveal a closet. A whole other bedroom lay before him, with a double bed and pretty floral-print curtains on the window. The sunshine coming in the window made a flat, bright, distorted rectangle on the peach-colored rug.

This was a much more cheerful place than Momma's old room, he thought. Momma's room seemed abandoned, with a frayed blanket on the bed and too many lamps standing around, as if they'd gotten lost and had wandered in and forgotten to leave.

He stepped cautiously into the perfect room, quietly closing the door. No stray socks on the floor or crooked pictures on the walls. The bedspread looked like it covered a bed in a store. Like a showroom, he thought. Maybe this was a guestroom. He'd heard that term somewhere. Maybe Tanya had used it. Or Batty Betty. She'd said she had to change the sheets on the bed in her guestroom before her niece came to visit.

But if this was the guestroom, why hadn't Momma slept in it? Or he and Angela? Maybe Grandma and Grandpa didn't think of them as guests. They were family. That made sense. He walked to the dresser and stared at the pictures stuck around the mirror. Small, smiling faces. Of boys and girls. Well, older than that. Teenagers.

"T.J.! Where are you?" Momma's voice sounded annoyed. He turned and retraced his steps, opening the door to find his mother just coming out of the room where he'd slept.

"Oh," Momma said. "I see you've discovered *the* room."

"I thought it was a closet," he said defensively.

"No. My old room serves that purpose. If I were you, I'd stay out of this room. Close the door, T.J. That's the way she wants it. Going in there will just get you in trouble."

"I can't find my sneakers," T.J. said. He stepped into the hallway and shut the door harder than necessary.

"Did you look under the bed? Angela was hiding there this morning, and she probably shoved them way in the back."

Momma had guessed right. After retrieving the missing sneakers and putting them on, T.J. followed her into the kitchen. Angela was sitting on two telephone books, drawing a picture with broken crayons she was selecting from a cookie tin full of them.

"You had a good night's sleep," said Grandma. "How about some pancakes for the big boy? How old are you, T.J.? Eight?"

"No, seven and a half."

"So, do you want seven and a half pancakes?" This time Grandpa spoke. He was sitting at the table, a cup of coffee in front of him and a newspaper folded beside it.

"I ... I don't think I can eat that many," T.J. said.

Grandpa chuckled. "I'm just teasing you. Eat as many as you'd like."

Grandma flipped two pancakes onto a blue plate. "Say when," she said.

"That's enough," said T.J. quickly, worried that this might be a clean-your-plate kind of home. He really wasn't very hungry.

"Maybe I'll make a cake today," said Grandma. "What kind of cake do you like best, T.J.?"

As he tried to think of an answer, Angela tossed a crayon back into the cookie tin and said, "I absotively love birthday cake!"

Grandma looked at her. "*Absotively?*"

"She's just speaking Angelese," T.J. explained.

Grandpa smiled and said, "You're absolutely positive?"

T.J. wasn't sure how to answer, so he shrugged as he sat down on a chair next to Angela.

"Well, it's not *anyone's* birthday, or is it?" Grandma gave a sharp glance at Momma.

"No," Momma said. "Angela's birthday is exactly one week before T.J.'s. In August."

"Oh, dear!" said Grandma. "So, do you two kids just share a big cake? Do you like the same kind? Chocolate? Yellow?"

"I like pink," said Angela. "Pink inside and … chartreuse outside."

"Chartreuse?" Grandma laughed. "You've got quite a vocabulary."

"I like chocolate cake," T.J. said. The only birthday cake he remembered had been at that foster home.

Momma was drinking coffee now and smiling a lot, so he decided not to mention birthdays. But Momma said, "When Angela was born, and I came home with her, T.J. was so excited! I'd told him that the baby was his birthday present. Just a few days early. Right before his fourth birthday. That first night, I woke up and the bassinet was gone. Not just the baby gone—the whole dang thing. I found it, with Angela still in it, next to T.J.'s bed, both of them sound asleep."

T.J. had heard this story before. Momma sometimes told it to him when he was disgusted with Angela. He wasn't sure he remembered doing that—moving the bassinet, dragging it all the way to his room. But since Grandma was giving him a kind look, he nodded.

"*I* was the best present T.J. ever got," said Angela, almost singing the words.

"How sweet is that?" Grandma said.

T.J. swallowed a mouthful of pancakes soaked with sugary syrup as he watched Angela. She had started a new drawing, and he realized it was of a birthday cake with way more than enough candles for their next combined birthdays. She looked so comfortable. As if she'd spent lots of mornings at Grandma and Grandpa's house, eating pancakes and drawing pictures.

He wished he could be like Angela.

"Well, it's Monday," said Grandpa, "and I have to head

off to work. You'll be the man of the house today, T.J. So have a good breakfast and a good day."

T.J. felt uneasy at the thought of Grandpa leaving. But his worries proved unfounded. The day went fine.

Looking back, he thought they'd probably had at least a month of fine days at their grandparents'. But time was funny. Maybe it had been longer.

One morning, while T.J. was still in bed, he heard the rumble of angry voices. Angela was asleep, her body curled under the blanket. Only wisps of her light hair stuck out. T.J. decided not to wake her.

Grandma had opened their bedroom window the night before. "Just a few inches," she'd said, "to let in some fresh air, and so you'll be able to smell the lilacs."

As T.J. climbed from bed, he caught the sweet scent of the tiny purple flowers that covered the bush outside the window. He headed toward the kitchen.

Grandpa was saying, "Now girls, just relax. I'm sure we can work something out."

T.J. stopped. He rested his fingers against the hallway wall, as if to steady himself.

"That's it, Allan, take her side." Grandma's words were as tart as lemon juice. "You always have. No wonder she grew up like ... this."

"Margie, now I don't think—"

"No, Allan, stop trying to make things work. It's not going to work. It never has. I tried so hard with you, Celia. What did I do wrong?"

"Just forget it, Mom." T.J. could just barely hear his mother's voice.

"No! I won't forget it!" Grandma was getting louder. "You made our lives a living hell, young lady. And now you come waltzing back. With two kids! And expect us to just drop everything and make things better for you?"

"Mom! You are so unfair! I don't expect *anything* from you."

"Oh, *right*. Just a roof and food and getting that junky old car of yours fixed and care for those children. You haven't even bothered to register your son at school. He's missing out on an education."

"Ah, Mom, he's just in second grade. It's almost the end of the year anyhow."

Grandma went on as if she hadn't heard. "And I suppose you'll expect me to babysit when—*if*—you ever get yourself a job. And where's their father, for heaven's sake? Or should I say 'fathers'? Do they even have the same one?"

"That's none of your business!" Momma's voice was cracking.

"Margie, Celia!" Grandpa said firmly. "You'll wake the children."

"You don't understand how hard it is, Mom. You had it easy, what with Dad here to help. I'm all alone with two kids …" Momma began to sniffle.

"That's it," said Grandma. "Start crying. That'll get *his* sympathy but not mine. You have always been the most manipulative and self-centered girl, Celia. You think the world owes you. Well, it doesn't. You need to take care of yourself. And your kids!"

"Mom! I *have* taken care of them. All these years, I haven't asked you for one thing!"

"We would have been happy to help. But you—you never even called us," Grandma said.

"I did call!"

"Yes, when T.J. was born. When was that? Over seven years ago! No letters. No cards. No calls. How do you think that makes me feel, Celia? I never even knew you had that little girl."

"And now that you know, you don't want her here," Momma said bitterly.

"That's not true! I just asked you a simple question. 'When are you going to go job hunting?' And that's what started all of this." Grandma sounded tired suddenly.

"Oh, no. *This* all started a long, long time ago, Mom. When I was just a kid. And you never had time for me. I was the 'difficult' one, remember? That's what you used to tell all your friends and relatives. That I was 'difficult.'"

"Celia, that was a long time ago. I don't even remember."

"That's just it, Mom. *You* don't remember, but *I* do!"

Now Grandpa spoke up. "Maybe you were a little more spunky, but we loved you, honey. We still love you. And your kids too."

"Well, you have a funny way of showing it. I'm barely here before Mom's yapping at me about getting a job. And acting like there's not enough room in this house. When all you'd have to do is open the door to that—that *shrine*, and let the kids sleep in there. Then I wouldn't have to spend my nights on the couch."

There was complete silence for a moment. T.J. held his breath.

Grandma's voice was strained when she finally spoke. "That room is off limits."

"Off limits? That room is such a cliché. Really. It's pathetic!" Momma said.

"A cliché?" Grandma's voice was shrill. "And I suppose your so-called life is brimming with originality?"

"Margie," Grandpa said, "don't say such things."

"Allan! You know how I feel about that room. It's all … all I have left of her."

"Her! *Her?*" Momma yelled. "You can't even say her name, can you? Becky! Becky! Becky! See? I can say it."

Grandpa said, "Celia, that's enough."

"No, Dad, it's not! Mom never got over how her *perfect* daughter got herself killed in a stupid car wreck. She thought it should have been me. Admit it, Mom! You wish *I'd* gotten killed instead of Becky. Right? Isn't that right?"

T.J. heard a crash in the kitchen and then loud footsteps. He barely had time to back against the wall before his grandmother came through the doorway and dashed past him and down the hallway. The sound of her sobs seemed to reverberate in his head even after she'd slammed the door to her bedroom.

"Well …" Grandpa said. "You went too far, Celia."

9

That very day, Momma repacked all the stuff she'd dragged out of the boxes and bags. She told T.J. later, after they'd loaded the car and driven back to the city, that Grandpa had given her money for rent. "Piles of money, T.J. Enough for at least a year."

They stayed in a motel on the east edge of the city for a few weeks while Momma looked for an apartment. The room reeked of cigarette smoke and perfume, though Momma said the flowery scent was an overdose of air freshener. T.J. decided it was a rotten lilac smell.

Summer had crept up while they'd been at Grandma and Grandpa's, so after apartment hunting each day, they went swimming.

On the first day Momma groaned as they approached the chain-link fence surrounding the pool behind the motel. T.J. read the hand-lettered sign that had been attached to the gate: *Pool closed until further notice.*

"What's that supposed to mean?" Momma asked, flicking her towel at a wasp. "They probably won't get it fixed until next summer."

"There's water in the pool," said T.J.

"I wanna go swimming!" Angela grabbed the gate and shook it angrily.

"Look at that!" Momma said in delight. "It's our lucky day. See? That stupid padlock wasn't closed. Must be a sign!" She laughed as she shoved the gate open and Angela danced through.

"You sure it's okay?" T.J. asked.

"Of course not." Momma laughed and swatted his butt with her towel. "But what can they do? Order us to get outta the pool, right? Big whoop. Come on, T.J., don't act like Too Jumpy. Live a little!"

As T.J. went inside the fence, he noted that the water had a slightly greenish cast, and there were scummy puddles in shallow indentations in the concrete that surrounded the pool. But Angela was already splashing and giggling, so he dropped his towel and joined her.

Four days later, Angela began to doggy-paddle along the edges, often dipping her face under and spewing water when she came up for air. T.J. still hung out in the shallow end, wading back and forth, his shoulders toasting in the late-afternoon sun.

No one else disobeyed the sign and came out to the pool. T.J. was glad because he didn't want anyone, even total strangers, seeing that his not-quite-four-year-old baby sister could swim while he was too scared to put his head under water.

The apartment they finally found seemed huge to T.J. It had two bedrooms and a dishwasher. He kept wondering if Momma could really afford it. She'd put all the money from Grandpa in a bank account.

Now, as they sat in the office of the apartment complex, Momma showed the manager a little book the bank had given her.

"You have a nice nest egg there, young lady." The man smiled and nodded, then pushed the booklet back across the shiny, black desk toward Momma.

"I've been building up this savings account for a while," she said with a modest tilt of her head. "And now, with this new job, I won't have to dip into it at all. I'll be assistant manager at that new store in the strip mall over on Spruce Street. You know the one? It's called The Better Way?"

The man shook his head. "Can't say as I've heard of that."

"Oh?" Momma sounded surprised. "Well, it *is* brand-new. I think there's a whole bunch of them in the Chicago area. This is the first one here, though. Watch for publicity. The grand opening is in ten days. You'll have to stop by, and I'll give you a special discount." Momma smiled and bent forward to reach for the savings account book on the desk.

"What sort of merchandise does it sell?" asked the apartment manager.

"They handle a ... variety. Actually, they have an assortment of apparel that's all handmade from organically grown materials," said Momma. "Their sweaters are out-of-this-world soft and gorgeous."

T.J. thought Momma was lying but wasn't sure.

Just then the man leaned over to open one of the desk drawers, and Momma glanced at T.J. and winked. He felt a giggle bubbling inside, so he rubbed his nose and looked at the floor. Angela was playing with one of her princess dolls, making it walk by bouncing its tiny feet along the arm of her chair.

The manager man sat up straight behind the desk and smiled at Momma. His teeth looked too big for his lips, and one strand of hair was sitting on the upper edge of the frames of his glasses, although he had a spot on top of his head that had no hair at all.

Momma smiled back at him and crossed her legs. She was

wearing a short skirt and her pretty tangerine shoes with the straps that went partway up her tan legs. Angela was sucking on a lollipop that the man had given her as they walked back to his office after he'd shown them the apartment. T.J. had been offered one too, but the only color the guy had was purple, and T.J. didn't like grape-flavored anything.

"And there's off-street parking," the man said.

"Oh, that's good." Momma nodded. "I'm getting a new car soon, so I'd rather not have it out on the street to get a ding in it."

"New car?" Angela grinned around her lollipop.

They got back to the motel room early that day, and Momma was happy. "By next year I'll have a job and I'll be on my feet," she said as if she meant it. "Today we should celebrate getting away from that old witch."

At first T.J. wasn't sure who she was talking about. Then he realized and decided that it wasn't fair for Momma to call Grandma a witch, but he was happy to see Momma in such a good mood.

Their celebration consisted of eating six candy bars from the motel vending machine and being able to spend the rest of the day in the pool. The sun was still high in the sky as they spread their towels on the bright, hot concrete next to the water. Momma sat in a deck chair in the shade of the building and opened a paperback book.

T.J.'s bare feet felt as if they were being roasted.

"Who wants cooked toes for a snack?" he asked, holding one foot in the air.

"Cut one off and I'll eat it," Angela said with a giggle as she scampered toward the edge of the pool.

"Watch where you step," T.J. said with authority. He'd

noticed that the puddles on the concrete had all dried up, leaving ugly stains. "Those spots are poison!"

"No they're not," said Angela, but she avoided stepping on the one in front of her. She hopped over it and leaped into the water.

"Look at me," T.J. said, prancing from one puddle stain to the next. "I'm king of the dark spots! Watch out, or I'll turn you into my puddle princess!"

"No! No! I don't want to be a puddle princess!" Angela shrieked in fake terror and used her hands to slosh water at his feet.

T.J. chased her across the shallow end, but she paddled away into deep water where he was afraid to follow. "Puddle Princess!" he yelled at her.

The sun was so intense that T.J. retreated to the shade, but he kept watch on his sister's antics.

By that night, Angela's shoulders and face were an alarming, brilliant red, and she was whining about how her skin hurt.

"You're fine," Momma said. "Hell, I had a burn so bad one time, when I went boating with my boyfriend on Lake Michigan, I got blisters all over my face."

"I don't want blisters! I absotively hate blisters!" Angela cried, even though T.J. was pretty sure she had no idea what blisters were.

Momma filled the bathtub with lukewarm water and gave Angela a bath. When it was time to get out, Angela complained so loudly, T.J. turned up the sound on the TV. The people in the room next door began pounding on the wall.

"Turn that thing down!" Momma yelled at him as she adjusted the air conditioning to its highest setting.

T.J. had to dig out an extra blanket from the dresser and wrap himself in it to keep his teeth from chattering, while Angela lay thrashing next to him on the bed, crying, "Too hot! Too hot!"

The next morning, they moved their meager belongings from the motel room into the apartment. Momma said that the guy who'd lent her money—the one T.J. called B.B.—had stolen all their furniture, but thanks to Grandpa's generosity, she was able to buy new things that were way better than their other stuff.

The first week in the apartment, Angela cried a lot. Her sunburn was a dull color by now and beginning to peel in ugly patches. But that wasn't what upset her. She cried because she'd gotten mixed up and thought they were leaving the motel to go back to their grandparents' house. "I want Grandpa to read me that story about the bear with a little brain," she'd say. Or, "Why can't Grandma come give me a good-night kiss?"

She didn't throw tantrums, exactly, but she whimpered and whined and cried. That got on T.J.'s nerves, and he poked at her peeling sunburn with one finger and said, "You look like a moldy strawberry, Puddle Princess."

"I am not a puddle princess!" Angela yelled.

"Shut up!" Momma ordered both of them. T.J. grabbed his raggedy baby blanket off the couch and ran into the kitchen. Angela cried harder until Momma smacked her face.

T.J. wished for a piece of quiet.

After that day, Angela began ducking and screaming as soon as their mother raised her hand. Finally she seemed to make the connection and quit asking about their grandparents. Or maybe she just forgot.

10

His stomach makes a funny gurgling sound as if it's talking to him. T.J. remembers that when he was little, Momma told him that a creature named T.J., for Tiny Jaguar, lived down there and needed to be fed. He puts one hand into his pocket and touches the coins that Marlene gave him, but he doesn't get up to buy food.

T.J. closes his life book and looks around the waiting room. To his surprise, none of the same people are there. The scene has shifted and changed while he's been looking at his life book. It's as if he left the room, was gone for a while. Gone into the past. Usually he doesn't think much about his "other life." That's what Marlene calls the time before he and Angela were placed for adoption with Marlene and Dan.

"Now you have a family, a *real* family," Marlene always says. "Now you don't have to worry about everything that happened in your other life, T.J., because Dan and I will take care of you. Stop worrying."

When Marlene says that, it reminds him of Momma. "Stop worrying, T.J.," Momma often said. "If you're not Too Jumpy, you must be Terribly Jittery! Maybe *that's* what T.J. stands for."

She always said it in a teasing, joking tone, and then she'd wink at him. He didn't mind when Momma said silly things about his name. It was fun, her talking to him as if his name was special.

T.J. sighs now—a useless noise, Momma used to tell him.

He yanks his life book open again. He's looking at page four. It shows a picture, made from yellow construction paper, of the sun. Above the picture are the words *The Ray Summer*. He remembers how he cut narrow strips of orange to make the rays of the sun. Every day with Ray was sunny. No, that couldn't be true. But that's how it seemed.

He notices for the first time that his life book skips right over the time they spent with their grandparents. He thinks of one of Momma's sayings, "Some things are best forgotten." But it's impossible to *choose* which things to forget and which things to remember.

He smoothes his fingers across the plastic covering of page four in his life book. Then he squints down at the sun picture, wishing it gave off heat like the real sun. The waiting room is chilly, the air clammy and stale, and he thinks he can taste disinfectant on his lips.

THEN—

Way before the Ray Summer, Momma used up all the money that Grandpa had given her. She'd said there was enough for a year, but it lasted just a few months. They moved out of the nice big apartment into a place above a downtown store that was "the size of a shoebox," according to Momma. She found a job as a waitress, which she "totally detested," but T.J. and Angela liked the leftovers she brought home, mostly desserts in clear plastic containers. Half a cherry pie, slices of chocolate cake that were crusty and stale-tasting on the edges but delicious in the middle, tapioca or vanilla pudding with a skin on top.

That winter, T.J. went to school, third grade, off and on. Momma overslept a lot because she was working part-time at night, and T.J. didn't wake up to catch the school bus. He often stayed up late, watching TV in an attempt to be awake when Momma got home. She was due in the house at 12:30 a.m., but usually she had extra jobs to do and didn't make it.

"Don't wait up for me," she always said, but he tried anyhow. So he was tired even on the days he made it to school. The classroom was warm, and the kids were quiet, busy, unlike his second-grade room in that other school. When he put his head down, he liked to breathe in the plastic smell of the top of his desk. He felt safe, making a secret place for his face within his folded arms.

One day Mrs. Herman talked to him during lunchtime recess when there were just a few other kids in the room, ones who had not done their homework and needed to do it in their free time. His teacher's voice was insistent but soft, even when he looked down and didn't answer her questions.

"Is anything wrong at home, T.J.? I need to know why you're missing so much school."

T.J. looked hard at his shoes. They were getting too small, and if he wiggled his big toes, he could see bumps where his feet were trying to poke holes and escape.

"Are you really sick so much?"

T.J. knew Mrs. Herman was accusing Momma of lying on those notes she wrote and sent with him to school. He didn't want to get his mother in trouble. She'd instructed him not to tell a soul, not a policeman or a teacher or anyone, that she was leaving him and Angela alone while she went to work. Momma said they'd take him and Angela away again if they knew. That he'd have to be a big boy and help her out.

So, forcing his eyes off his feet to stare at his teacher, he said, "Yeah, I get sick a lot. I have ..." He tried to think of some impressive illness that would explain his problems. But he could tell, looking up at Mrs. Herman's wrinkly face, that she was not the sort of person who'd accept an offhand lie. "I have ... trouble waking up, sometimes. And Momma lets me sleep in. She's going to take me to the doctor soon."

"Soon?" Mrs. Herman said all this in a whisper, but T.J. could sense the punished kids, fiddling with their No. 2 pencils instead of working on their math problems, listening to the teacher quiz him.

He nodded quickly and hard so there'd be no mistake. "She's taking me to see the doctor on Tuesday." He made a mental note to be absent on Tuesday.

But when he tried to stay home, Momma got mad at him. "You have school, T.J. Get up!"

"I can't. It's Tuesday."

"So? That's a school day. Or do you have it off? Is it another one of those idiotic Teacher Days or something?" She stomped off into the kitchen area, and he could hear her pulling out the drawer where she stored the school calendar.

"T.J.! Get your butt up off that couch. You have school. You gotta go to school. They'll send out the authorities again if you don't go. They came last week while you were at school. Woke me and Angela up. Gave me all sorts of crap about what a lousy mother I am. That's not what they said, but I could tell that's what they thought. What do they expect? Keep cutting welfare, expect me to work and take care of two kids at the same time? By the way, don't forget. I never leave you at home alone, right?"

T.J. sat up and swung his feet to the floor. "No, Momma, you never leave us alone."

"Good boy!" She came over and kissed the top of his head. Momma looked so pretty, leaning over him, her hair hanging loosely over the shoulders of her pink waitress uniform with her name on a card tucked into a plastic case and pinned to her pocket. *Celia*, it read in a pretty, swirly script. Angela murmured in her sleep, and when Momma reached out and touched her, she curled into a ball like one of those fuzzy caterpillars. Her thumb was stuck in her mouth.

"I love you, T.J.," Momma said softly, and yawned. "Have a good day at school," she added as she turned toward the bedroom. He realized then that she'd just gotten home, even though her shift was over at midnight.

So he went to school that Tuesday, prepared to tell Mrs. Herman that his doctor's appointment had been changed, but she didn't ask.

That was about all he recalled of third grade. He shoved away the memories of the fifth-grade boys who slammed him up against the walls and made him pull out his pockets and hand over the contents. He got free lunches, so his pockets usually held junk rather than money. The older boys jeered at whatever he held out to them—a piece of string, a brown pebble, three pennies. Then they laughed and slapped his hands so that he dropped everything. "Don't touch that stuff!" said the tallest boy. "It's covered with foster boy fungus!" That kid made it sound like the worst insult.

T.J. wanted to scream, "I'm not a foster boy," but he knew it wouldn't help. Somehow they knew that he had been in a foster home. One of the boys had an aunt who worked in the school office. Maybe she'd read T.J.'s records and then blabbed about them to the boy's mom.

He was glad when summer vacation arrived, even though Momma usually slept most of the day. She seemed to feel guilty about that and tried to be extra nice when she was awake. There was a Dairy Queen nearby, and one day, after she'd slept until mid-afternoon, they went there and had a late lunch. Angela ate a chocolate sundae and a large vanilla cone.

Because of that day of unlimited ice cream, according to Momma, Angela developed a sweet tooth. T.J. wondered which one of Angela's itty-bitty teeth was the sweet one.

Often, when she smiled, he would point and yell, "There it is! I see your sweet tooth!" And she would giggle and stick out her tongue. Or, depending on her mood, she might clamp her mouth shut and glare at him.

Angela reminded him of Momma sometimes.

The summer heat was like another body in their tiny apartment, breathing out moist air and taking up space.

"I wanna go to D.Q. It's too hot here!" Angela would start as soon as Momma got up.

And Momma's answer was always the same. "Oh, not again, Angela. I can't take you to Dairy Queen every single day."

"Go D.Q.!"

"No, you'll get fat! You don't want to be fat and ugly like that stupid Tanya, do you?" Momma asked.

T.J. didn't think Angela remembered who Tanya was, although she used the name 'Tupid Tanya for her oldest doll with the broken-off arm and left her lying around naked on the floor.

Soon Angela's whines for a Dairy Queen trip would turn to shrieks, and if that didn't work, she'd have a real tantrum.

Angela's tantrums were impressive. First she'd yell and shake her head so that her long, wispy hair flew out in a deranged halo. Then she'd pound her fists on whatever was handy. Soon she'd be on the floor, with all her arms and legs going every which way, hitting whatever was nearby, including anyone who ventured too close.

Momma wanted to spank Angela, T.J. was sure. She'd have her squinty, evil-eyed look, and her lips would stretch real thin, and she'd put one hand up in the air above Angela's writhing body. But then she'd stop and stomp away.

He remembered being spanked himself, lots and lots of times. But ever since those people had come to see Momma about him missing school, she was holding back. When Angela was having a tantrum, often T.J. wished Momma would just beat her little butt and get it over with.

Instead, finally, Momma would scream above Angela's noise, "Stop acting like a baby! You're four years old!"

Angela simply yelled louder with her four-year-old lungs.

"Okay!" Momma would scream back at her. "We'll go, for God's sake!"

Angela always kept up the tantrum a little longer, as if she wanted to make "absotively" sure she'd won.

11

Each time they entered the Dairy Queen, T.J. braced himself, but the cold air was always a shock, hitting his sweaty skin hard. It felt just like when one of the older kids at that blue-house foster home had turned a hose on him. Icy-cold water blasting his whole body full force.

Momma reminded them that money was tight, so they never ordered anything but cones. Angela seemed to sense that begging for seconds would have tipped their mother over the edge.

Dairy Queen was a daily treat, and T.J. loved it just as much as Angela. Then one of the guys behind the counter began to talk to Momma. His name was Ray, and he had short blond hair and a fuzzy growth above his top lip that was trying to be a mustache. Soon Ray was coming over to visit at the apartment. Momma always acted surprised when Ray showed up, and he'd dip his head, looking shy.

T.J. liked Ray because he acted more like a kid than a grownup most of the time. He would toss Angela up in the air, and she'd laugh until she got hiccups. And when Ray teased Angela about sucking her thumb, she didn't get mad.

"What flavor is that thumb of yours today?" Ray asked each afternoon when he arrived. The first time, Angela wouldn't play along. She stood there with her thumb plugged in, silent, but with the corners of her mouth turned up. "Vanilla? Strawberry?" Ray asked.

Finally she reacted, giggling, waving her shriveled thumb in the air. "Today it's chocolate chip cookie dough," she said.

The next day it was lemon sauce with cream. From then on, Ray made three guesses every day but never got it right, because Angela's pretend flavors were impossible to predict.

"She'll never quit sucking her thumb with you around," Momma complained, but her face shone with its special Ray smile.

Ray liked to cook, and he made lasagna and huge salads with crunchy, strange nuts in them. He told Momma that they all needed to get out more, and he convinced her to come along to the park and to the nearest city swimming pool, where he taught T.J. to swim.

T.J. remembered that summer more clearly than any other because each day with Ray was a special flavor. When he moved in with them, Momma quit her job, and life seemed slow and happy.

Ray bought a mammoth fan for their non-air-conditioned, second-floor apartment and installed it in the living room window, which was shaded by the spreading branches of an ancient oak tree. With the fan turned on high, a refreshing whoosh of air brought in a cool, summery scent even on the hottest days. And at night T.J. and Angela would lie on the big fold-out couch with the whir of the fan and the breeze making sleep come easily.

The best part about Ray was how he affected Momma. She laughed a lot that summer. T.J. still had some clear memories of Ray. Like snapshots, or maybe more like short little DVDs that he could play over and over in his mind.

One day Ray drove all of them to Walnut Park, way across town. His car was small, with hardly any room in the back seat, but Ray insisted that he and Angela wear their seatbelts. Momma was laughing in the front, tossing her hair over the back of her seat, and Angela reached out and stroked the long strands with the tips of her fingers.

"This is some car, Ray!" Momma said. "Seems just right for picking up girls. But you've already got your girl."

Ray glanced in the rear-view mirror and winked at T.J. "How do you think I got you, Celia?"

"Oh, no! Not the *car*! I didn't even know you owned a car when I first met you at the Dairy Queen. I didn't know you were a little rich boy."

"I'm not a little boy," Ray said sternly, reaching out and touching Momma's bare knee.

Momma laughed. "Maybe it's time you traded in this girl-catcher and got something practical. More fitting to a family man. Unless this is just a summer romance." Momma's tone was light, but T.J. sensed that she was serious.

It was Ray's turn to laugh as he swung the car around a corner too sharply, sending T.J. leaning against the side. Angela giggled and waved her hands. "Do that again!" she cried.

Was that the day they roasted marshmallows over a charcoal grill and went on the merry-go-round at the very center of the park? Or maybe those things happened on other days.

T.J. had never eaten anything quite like the marshmallows—crisp and warm on the outside, soft like a magic cloud on the inside, with a taste so tender and sweet that he kept eating them until he felt sick.

And he'd gotten his pick of the horses on the merry-go-round. It was twilight, and the park was nearly empty. Fireflies danced through the air, winking like Christmas lights that had escaped to summertime. No bigger kids were around to tease him for going on a kiddie ride. So he climbed on the blackest horse with fiery red nostrils and shiny hoofs and a hard mane that he pretended was whipping his face as they twirled around and around. Angela was next to him on the cream-colored horse, squealing with delight like some baby. But Momma, who was sitting sideways on the horse behind him, had eyes only for Ray, standing beside her, his arms wrapped protectively around her waist.

One day, in the apartment, Ray showed them how to make a kite out of newspaper, long, slender sticks of wood, string, and glue. Then they all—even Momma—went to the nearby school playground to fly it.

Angela sobbed when the kite crashed and broke, and T.J. was sure she was on the edge of a tantrum. But when they got home Ray found a thin sheet of paper and demonstrated how to fold it into the shape of a bird.

"A paper crane," Ray said as he held it up high and let go, so it swooped down on the breeze from the fan. T.J. lost interest when he found the birds hard to make, but Angela was clever at folding each piece of paper just so. She made five cranes that afternoon and hardly sucked her thumb at all.

Every Saturday morning Ray took T.J. and Angela to the library, and they came home with a huge stack of books. Most of the time Ray read aloud to them, his voice slipping into that of each character as easily as changing socks. Some of the books were fat with hardly any pictures. Ray sometimes listened to T.J. read and encouraged him to sound out the difficult words. Momma would say, "Oh, he's a smart one, that T.J."

"What's 'T.J.' stand for?" Ray asked one day.

"Tom Jones," Momma said with a short laugh. "He's named for his father, first and last name. But I gave him my last name in the hospital for good measure. Because by that time ol' Tom Jones was long gone. He was a wimp. Couldn't handle anything, that Tom Jones."

T.J. had never met his father and didn't think he ever would. But being named for him made T.J. feel a small connection with the vanished Tom Jones.

Ray grinned at T.J. "You have the perfect name. It sounds mysterious. You don't have to tell people what the initials stand for. You're just T.J."

T.J. nodded.

Ray acted a lot like a father. Even better than the foster dad in the blue house.

But then, near the end of the summer, everything changed.

The morning air was cool as it came in through the fan. T.J. was eating a bagel with cream cheese and watching TV, sitting on the floor with his favorite blanket wrapped around his bare legs. Momma was in the kitchen area, which was really just an extension of the living room. She was making pancakes for Ray, who hadn't gotten up yet. Angela was at the table, kneeling on her chair. Her breakfast trash was spread over half the table. Using jelly like finger paint, she was smearing an intricate floral design on her plate.

The doorbell rang. It startled T.J. because it hadn't worked most of the time they'd lived in this apartment. Ray had fixed it just the week before.

Momma turned off the burner and went to the door, wiping her hands on her T-shirt, which was all she was wearing over a pair of panties. She peered through the peephole and frowned. T.J. felt a vague uneasiness and gripped the edge of his old blanket, trying to find the smooth spot that was soothing to stroke.

He glanced toward Angela, and their eyes met. She slid off her chair and came toward him, her thumb in her mouth.

"Hello?" said a high-pitched voice through the closed door. "Is anyone home? I'm here to deliver this check. You won that contest at Heflen's Jewelry."

T.J. could see Momma hesitate. She turned from the door and looked at T.J. "Did Ray enter some contest at that jewelry store downtown?" She was talking softly, still trying to pretend they weren't home even though the television was turned up loud.

In answer, T.J. shrugged. Momma imitated his motion. She looked again through the peephole. "Well," Momma said quietly to T.J., "it's some lady who's got what looks like an envelope. I guess there's no harm in checking this out."

After that, his memories of what happened were all mixed up. Suddenly there was this strange lady inside their apartment, and Momma was screaming at her and trying to push her back out into the hallway.

"Raymond!" the woman screeched. "You come out of that bedroom now!"

And then a man came through the door. His face was the color of the beets Ray had coaxed T.J. to eat one night at dinner. This man was breathing hard. He had a mustache, yellow and thick, but hardly any hair on top of his head. He was yelling too.

"We're spending good money for you to go to college! You're not going to throw it all away on *this mess*." The man gestured with a large hand, taking in the whole apartment with one sweep. T.J. felt as if he himself were part of the mess, along with a couple of pizza boxes from the night before, three or four pop cans, and scattered piles of books and toys.

The woman had taken a newspaper clipping from the envelope and was waving it in Momma's face. "He's engaged! To a wonderful girl."

Momma stopped screaming and grabbed the piece of paper, glanced at it, then crumpled it in her fist. She began to cry.

Angela clutched T.J.'s hand. She kept asking, "What's wrong? What's the matter? What's happening?" But T.J. had no answers. Angela's fingers were jam-covered and sticky and hot.

Then Ray was in the kitchen, wearing only his underwear. He looked small and pale, and the man and the woman were telling him to pack his stuff. "The party's over!" the man said.

And it was. Ray left.

After that day Momma quit laughing. She didn't talk about Ray. Every time Angela asked for him, Momma said, "Shut up! Just shut up!" She got mad at T.J. over and over and blamed him when Angela got into things like her makeup. Or whenever Angela had a tantrum. "Why weren't you watching her?" Momma would ask. Or, "What did you do to her?"

Momma decided that they had to move because the shoebox apartment was too expensive. So they found another tiny place in a brick building in a junky part of town. Far away from the Dairy Queen. By then it was fall, and Momma said it was way too cold for ice cream.

12

T.J. shuts his life book and stares at the floor of the waiting room. There are scuffmarks, black ones, leading toward the doors that hide the examining room where Angela was taken so long ago. He wonders what could be happening to her. The cold pain in his gut has grown bigger and is pushing its way up into his throat.

Please wake up, Angela. Pretty please with sugar and whipped cream and a cherry and coconut ...

He tells himself not to cry.

"You're a tough kid," Dan has said to T.J. "You know, it's okay to cry sometimes, kiddo." T.J. likes Dan to call him "kiddo." It's lots better than being called Timothy. Which is not his name.

Now his life book feels heavy on his lap, as if the memories themselves have weight and are pressing on his knees. Another letter forms in his mind.

Dear Momma,

Remember that summer when Ray came and we were all happy? You told him I was named for my daddy, Tom Jones. Do you still think I'm a wimp like my daddy?

I wish you weren't dead. I could ask you about my daddy if you were alive.

  Your son,
  T.J.

He tried to tell Mrs. Cox about his name on the day they were making their life books. She was talking on and on about their upcoming move from foster care into a "real, forever" home.

"Marlene and Dan are so excited about becoming parents," Mrs. Cox said. She frowned at the paper crane taking shape in Angela's hands. "They will be just thrilled when you two are with them for good."

T.J. and Angela had not only met but even visited Marlene and Dan in their house with the huge backyard and swing set and wading pool. Angela had stared at the pool and said, "I already know how to swim. This is for babies."

"Shut up," T.J. had told her. Even though he wasn't at all sure whether he wanted Marlene and Dan to adopt him and Angela, he felt that insulting their pool was not a good idea.

But Marlene had frowned at him, not Angela, and said, "Timothy, we don't say 'shut up' in our house."

Everything about Marlene and Dan was different from what he was used to. T.J. wished he could feel excited about moving in with them, but he didn't.

And making this stupid life book was not helping.

"How come she calls me Timothy?" he asked Mrs. Cox. "My name's T.J. Not Timothy."

Mrs. Cox gathered up Angela's cranes and put them in a paper bag. She shook her head. "Your name is Timothy James Riley. Says so right in your records."

T.J. wished he could take those stupid records and throw them out a window way up high and let them flutter away and get lost like Angela's paper birds. "My name is T.J.," he said again.

"Yes, that's your nickname." Mrs. Cox smiled at him. "But your given name is Timothy James."

He wondered if she was planning on throwing that bag and those birds in the trash can. But he had more important concerns.

"T.J. That's my initials and my name. T.J. stands for Tom Jones. That was my daddy's name."

"Well, I'm sorry, T.J. You must be mistaken." Mrs. Cox set the bag of paper cranes on the table and pulled a folder out of her scuffed black briefcase. She riffled through the papers in the folder and then pulled out a 5 x 7 school picture and laid it on the table next to the paper bag. "See?"

He looked at the words where she was pointing. *Timothy James Riley* was typed on a label that had been stuck to the bottom of that photograph of himself.

Did Momma lie to him? Maybe she'd made up that business about him being named for his father. Maybe there was no Tom Jones anywhere.

"You know," Mrs. Cox said, "Marlene was so pleased to learn your name is Timothy. I heard her tell Dan that she always planned to name a baby boy Timothy." Mrs. Cox slid the picture back into the folder.

"I'm not a baby boy," T.J. said, feeling angry, suddenly, at Marlene because she had wanted a baby, not an eleven-year-old. "Can I see all that stuff? Those records?"

"Well, not really, T.J. I mean, most of this ... these papers are official, AFCS business. Not interesting at all."

"It's all stuff about me and Angela, right? And our momma."

"No. Not all of it." Mrs. Cox had shoved the folder back into her briefcase and was hooking the clasp.

"Please? Could I just see some of the stuff? I mean, you showed me that picture." T.J. felt as if those records were more important to some people than the real, live Angela and T.J. He wanted to see what was hidden inside that folder in the worst way. It suddenly seemed important. Worth being extra polite. "Please? Are there more pictures? I think that one you showed me was from second grade."

He could tell Mrs. Cox was relenting as she set her brief-case on the table.

"Let me check. Maybe I have a snapshot of your mother that Angela could put in her life book."

She didn't find any pictures of Momma, but there were two more school pictures of T.J. and one of Angela taken the year when she was in kindergarten. T.J. studied his own face but couldn't remember when the pictures had been taken. There was nothing written underneath or on the back of the first one he flipped over. So he looked on the back of the other picture.

T.J. Kindergarten was written in Momma's rounded cursive. And underneath that, someone (a social worker? a policeman?) had scrawled, in skinny, spiky letters, what looked like *Tim James*. Beneath that was printed, apparently by yet another official person, with a felt-tipped pen, *Timothy James*, and a question mark after it.

"Look," T.J. said to Mrs. Cox. He pointed to the scratchy Tim James writing. "I bet that's supposed to be Tom Jones. Somebody with sloppy handwriting wrote my name. And then somebody else guessed it was supposed to be Timothy James. But it's not. My name is T.J. Just T.J."

Keeping his real name, the one Momma had given him, was important to him, but he couldn't explain why.

"Oh, T.J., I'm sure there was no guessing about your

name!" Mrs. Cox peered at the writing on the back of the photo and shook her head. "Well, it does look a bit strange. I suppose something like that might happen. But what difference does it make? I mean, you are called T.J. whether your name is Timothy or Tom, right?"

"But she … Marlene … calls me Timothy. Lots of times, Dan does too."

Mrs. Cox looked flustered as she put the photos back into the folder and then her briefcase. "I'm sorry about that, T.J. I will mention it to them. But Marlene loves the name Timothy, and it seemed like such a nice coincidence. As if it was all meant to be."

T.J. opened his mouth to say that it wasn't "meant to be" if his name was not Timothy. But before he could say that, Angela jumped off her chair.

"I gotta go potty," she said loudly, and Mrs. Cox had to take her to the bathroom down the hallway.

By the time they came back, T.J. was working on another page in his life book. He was making a picture that was intended to upset his caseworker.

"Who's that?" Mrs. Cox asked him when she glanced at the picture.

"Billy," he answered.

"Well, he certainly isn't a very attractive person," Mrs. Cox said with a frown. "Are you sure you want to include him in your life book?"

"Why not?" asked T.J. "He's part of my life."

"Oh, well, I understand, but …" Her voice trailed off. "Angela? Please draw something, anything, for your life book. How many birds have you made? Six, is it? That's really plenty."

Angela's clear blue eyes drifted up from the yellow piece of paper she had just started to fold. Her gaze settled on T.J.'s drawing. "Billy?" she whispered.

T.J. covered the picture with both hands. He had not thought about Angela's noticing it. "You don't need to look at him. He was no good, remember?"

Angela nodded her head, her soft curls moving gently at the top of her shirt collar. But her face looked pinched up, as if she were holding something inside so no one would see it. T.J. wished he'd lied. Pretended it was someone else. Or not included Billy in his life book at all.

The picture actually looked nothing like Billy. It showed more how T.J. felt about him. Wild lines coming off the purple circle of a face. Huge eyes that stared out, as if to see all the things T.J. wanted to keep hidden, to keep safe. And growing out of that face were long arms with sharp fingernails.

Mrs. Cox let out a long sigh. "He looks like a monster."

13

T.J. wasn't sure when Billy had come. Probably a little after Christmas the year T.J. was in fourth grade and Angela in kindergarten. Momma had finally found a job, working as a receptionist at a big building downtown. T.J. was impressed when they went for a drive past it. There were so many windows he thought it'd take hours to count them all.

He liked the way Momma looked each morning when she was dressed for work. She wore fancy clothing, not jeans and sloppy shirts like Miss Carrie and Miss Mary. Those were the ladies who worked at the daycare center where Momma dropped him and Angela each morning. T.J. spent only about half an hour there before the school bus pulled up at the curb, right in front of Wee Care, at 7:48. The bus dropped him off at the same place after school.

He had few memories of daycare. There'd been so many other kids, so many toys, and so much noise. He remembered one good thing—with all the activity and the excitement of going to daycare plus afternoon kindergarten, Angela seemed to forget about having tantrums.

A whole day of fourth grade combined with daycare was exhausting, and each afternoon T.J. was relieved when Momma arrived to pick him and Angela up. On most days she was the last parent to get there, but she always gave Miss Carrie and Miss Mary a good excuse, and she talked in such a quick, breathless way, smiling and laughing as she gathered up Angela's stuff, that the daycare ladies never complained to her face.

But he heard them muttering sometimes, and saw them glancing at their watches. He told himself not to care. Momma was the prettiest mother, so it didn't matter if she was late. Sometimes she gave him a big hug when she arrived, and he was glad all the other kids were gone so he could hold on to her for a few seconds without having to worry that somebody would tease him. But usually Momma was in too much of a hurry to take time for hugs.

T.J. first suspected that there was another man in their mother's life the day he and Angela climbed into the back seat of the car and Momma announced, "I'm gonna quit that stupid job."

He was trying to untangle Angela's seatbelt. He always sat in the back next to her because Momma had so much junk on the front seat. Bottles of spring water, her huge brown purse, wrappers from fast-food places. Momma never liked to wait for him to get Angela situated, and now his little sister was whining and squirming with her thumb in her mouth. She knew perfectly well how to hook her own seatbelt, but she refused to do it. Often Angela fell asleep on the short ride home. On this day, he could tell from the glazed look in her eyes that she was very tired.

"How come you gonna quit?" he asked Momma.

"Oh, I get no respect. Those people all think they're way better than me. All those executive types, trying to make me feel bad about myself. I got good grades in school, T.J. At least until seventh grade. But those people act like I'm retarded. I just won't take it. That Mr. Conners, he's the worst." T.J. knew that Mr. Conners was Momma's boss.

A few days later, she stopped going to work in the windowed building. A week after that, Billy moved in.

"He's like B.B.," said T.J. to Momma after Billy had been living with them for about a week.

"Who?" Momma was brushing her hair at the bathroom sink. T.J. was standing over the toilet, trying to pee, but he was embarrassed with his mother right there next to him. When he'd asked her to leave, she'd laughed and said, "I've wiped your little butt so many times, T.J. Don't worry about showing anything to me."

"Billy," answered T.J. "Billy's like B.B." He felt safe saying this because Billy had just gone out to get pizza.

"Boy, you are talking nonsense. Who the hell is B.B.?"

"That guy. The one who was always kissing you that you didn't like." T.J. was sure Momma had not forgotten the man who stole their furniture while they were with their grandparents.

"T.J., a lot of guys have kissed me that I didn't like. You keep that in mind when you get a little bit older. Positively no kissing girls unless they want to be kissed. And you're way wrong about Billy. He's very sweet to me, and I love kissing him. Now I'm done with my hair, and I'm leaving so you can have some privacy. Pee in peace, T.J."

"He took all our nice furniture 'cause you couldn't pay him, remember?"

"Oh. *Him.* Some things—and I do mean *things*—are best forgotten." Momma leaned over and gave him a kiss on the top of his head.

"Momma! Stop that!"

She giggled and wiggled her fingers at him as she left the bathroom.

That night Billy came home with some friends. They sat

at the kitchen table playing cards, eating, and drinking. And swearing as easily as they breathed. Especially Billy. Momma sat with them, close to Billy, even though it was all guys, no other women.

T.J. liked having company because it made his mother laugh. He and Angela were watching TV in the living room, which in this apartment was almost on top of the kitchen. It was a Saturday night, so no one told them to go to bed. And since their bed was the couch, there was no point. A commercial came on with a loud, jingly tune that always made T.J. want to smile.

"Turn it down!" Billy ordered.

T.J. leaped up and jabbed at the volume control on the TV. The remote had been lost for days. He accidentally hit it the wrong way, and a blast of music crashed into the room. T.J. was so startled he jumped back as if the TV had bitten him.

Billy swore and lunged out of his chair. T.J. almost felt him coming and shrank back on the couch, clutching a small red pillow in front of his face.

But Billy just turned down the volume, growling, "Kids! Make a man wanna drink."

One of Billy's friends laughed and said, "I'll drink to that."

T.J. peered over the pillow at Billy, who scowled at him and said, "What's the matter with you?"

T.J. shrugged.

Billy imitated him, shrugging his massive shoulders and scrunching up his face as if he was terrified and about to cry. After a round of approving laughter from his friends, Billy said, "You better start to man up or *somebody's* gonna give you a reason to cry."

"He's not crying," Angela said as she bounced on the

couch, adding to the sick feeling that was stirring inside T.J.'s stomach.

Billy said, "Listen to this little punkin. Now *she's* a fighter. Take a lesson from your baby sister, kid, or the whole world is gonna think you're a dumb-ass."

As Billy stomped back to the table, T.J. curled himself into a ball around the pillow. Despite what Angela had said, he could feel tears in his eyes, and his nose was running. He used the pillow to swipe at the snot. This was the pillow that Billy always tucked under his head when he sat on the couch to watch TV.

Angela wrinkled her nose. "Yuck! Momma, T.J.'s blowing his nose all over the red pillow!"

"Oh, come on!" Momma said. "Stop that, T.J. You two, shut up. Quit tattling, Angela."

"*What'd* he do?" Billy's voice rose. He came back to the couch and snatched the pillow out of T.J.'s hands. "You li'l son of a ..."

Billy flung the pillow against the wall and grabbed T.J.'s arm above his elbow, then yanked him to the floor. "You keep doing dumb stuff like that, it'll be *me* who beats some sense into you."

"Let him go," interrupted Momma, who'd followed Billy the few steps into the living room. She picked up the red pillow. "I'll throw this away."

"Maybe we should throw *him* away too." Billy made sure his friends at the table heard him. Then he lifted T.J. by his arm and shoved him back onto the couch.

Several of the other men chuckled as if all this was a joke, but T.J.'s stomach clenched and he needed to pee right then.

Stumbling off the couch, he tried not to think about those men around the table, watching with their sharp eyes.

When he got to the bathroom, he swallowed a couple of times as he shut the door firmly. The lock was broken.

T.J. used the toilet and then zipped up his jeans.

His upper arm throbbed and his shoulder ached, but he told himself it was no big deal. He hadn't even gotten hit.

He sat down on the edge of the toilet seat because the lid was missing. His legs were trembling slightly.

Stupid legs, he thought.

T.J. tried to breathe evenly, counting. He'd gotten to forty-three when, suddenly, his stomach lurched, and he felt the sick taste of the pizza he'd eaten hours before. He turned around, sliding down onto his knees so he could hang his head over the toilet bowl.

When he'd finished vomiting, he reached for the toilet paper. The roll was empty. He got to his feet and went to the sink, where he splashed water over his face. Bits of vomit from his lips fell into the sink. He spent a long time washing it clean. Then he flushed the toilet.

Through the closed door, he heard Momma laughing.

14

Billy took over the whole apartment. His body was large. A bulldozer, thought T.J. And his voice was a jackhammer. But it wasn't just his physical presence and his noise. His things crowded and shoved against the few belongings of T.J.'s family. Billy brought suitcases of clothing and boxes of other stuff that were soon stacked along the walls. A few of the boxes looked new and had pictures of products on the outside.

"Don't touch anything," Billy warned T.J. and Angela. But when Billy wasn't home, T.J. studied those boxes. Radios and toasters. Microwave ovens and laptop computers, looking brand-new. The boxes didn't stay. Billy and his friends carried them out but soon brought in more, a round robin of stuff. T.J. guessed it was stolen.

A couple of Billy's friends came one late night, wearing uniforms of some sort. T.J. woke up and went to the bathroom. For a moment he thought the cops had come. Then he realized that the uniforms were the kind guards wore. People who were supposed to watch over buildings and keep the things inside them safe. Billy never wore a uniform, yet he seemed to be in charge. The boss.

The gnawing pain in T.J.'s stomach was constant.

But Momma was thrilled with the new blender and the shiny microwave on the counter. Now that she wasn't working, T.J. and Angela no longer went to Wee Care.

T.J. was surprised that he missed the routine of the day-care center. He'd always liked the stories Miss Mary read after school. Chapter books to the older kids, like *Charlotte's Web* and *Charlie and the Chocolate Factory* and *Hatchet*. He wondered if he would have had the courage to save Wilbur, the pig, the way that girl Fern did. If her father had been like Billy, even Fern would have failed. And he wished he could win something like Charlie. Just a candy bar would be a good enough prize for T.J. He loved *Hatchet*, but no way could he survive on his own out in the wilderness.

Sometimes T.J.'s mouth watered at the memory of the ice-cold chocolate milk and orange-colored crackers with smears of peanut butter that they had for snacks at Wee Care.

T.J. moved around the apartment cautiously, avoiding Billy's long arms and vise-like grip. Angela seemed fearless, and Billy rewarded her. He gave her the pet name of Punkin while he called T.J. a lot of other names. Mean names.

"Come sit up here, Punkin," Billy said one afternoon while Momma was out having her hair done. He was watching TV. Whenever Billy occupied the couch, there was no room for anyone else except Momma, who seemed to love cuddling up next to him.

Now Billy was lying with one foot sticking out, his head propped up on a blue pillow that Momma had bought to replace the red one.

Angela was on the floor next to T.J. in front of the TV. She was sucking her thumb. The show Billy was watching was about stuff that T.J. was sure would get him in trouble if he mentioned it at school. He knew better, but Angela, just in kindergarten, might not realize that repeating some things from TV got you sent to see the principal.

He'd tried to interest her in the comic book he was reading. But she seemed fascinated by the people on TV. There was nowhere else to go in the tiny apartment. Momma and Billy's bedroom was off limits that day, and anyway the TV in there wasn't working.

"Hey, Punkin, I'm talking to you."

T.J. heard the warning in Billy's voice, and he wanted to shake his little sister. *Run!* he almost said, but his mouth was dry, and he stared hard at the picture in his comic book— Spider-Man clinging to the side of a building. Whenever Billy used that tone and T.J. didn't respond quickly, Billy's long arms would reach out and grab him and force him to do whatever Billy wanted.

"You like that chick, Toady Jody?" Billy asked him, and T.J. knew he was talking about the blond woman on TV. She was telling the host about her husband, who had run off to live with her boyfriend.

Billy's voice got louder. "Your little sister will look like her someday, I bet."

"No," said Angela. "She's fat. I'm skinny. See?" Angela hopped up and pulled her shirt up to expose her stomach and ribs that stuck out, her pale skin stretched over them. She pulled her shirt down and returned her thumb to her mouth.

"Come over here, Punkin," Billy said as he sat up and patted one leg.

Without taking her eyes off the TV, Angela climbed onto Billy's knee. She balanced there, sucking her thumb, while Billy laid one hand on her back and muttered, "Let's see how wide—" Angela began to squirm and Billy grabbed her arm roughly. "Hold still! I wanna see just how skinny you are."

"Why?" asked T.J.

Billy's answer was harsh. "Get out of here, you nosy little cretin. Don't you have any friends? When I was your age, I was never home. Always on the streets, playing ball, shooting hoops, riding bikes. You name it."

T.J. scrambled up from the floor and tossed his comic book on the counter, then went out the door of the apartment. The hallway was filled with odors of meals cooked that day. The building had three floors. An old man lived in one of the other apartments on the second floor. T.J. always thought of him as the shadow man because he was so quiet and gray-looking. But one day the man had stopped T.J. as he came into the building, walking quickly as he always did after getting off the school bus. "Your daddy, he a fence or what?"

"He's not my father," T.J. said, ducking out from under the man's restraining arm. He hadn't seen the shadow man since.

On the top floor of the building, there were a couple of families from some other country. The greasy, spicy smell now drove T.J. onto the steps, where the air from below was fresher.

He had made up a game for stairs. It was something he could play all alone. He'd step down one step and then back up, switching feet in quick succession. It was fun, trying to go faster and faster, listening to the frantic, crazy tapping of his shoes. He had tried to teach Angela how to do it, but her feet didn't work as fast as his, and she got bored and never wanted to play.

There was another kid, a girl, who lived with one of the upstairs families. Last time he'd been playing alone on the steps, she'd come out and watched him from the top landing, peering around the railing. She had a small brown face and a mass of dark hair. Her expression had been serious as she stared at his feet. T.J. wondered later if she'd realized that he was looking at her, seeing her frown in concentration, as if she wanted to memorize the way his feet moved down and back up.

He'd overheard her mother calling to her in the hallway, so he was fairly sure her name was something like Iza. She didn't ride the bus with him, but she went to the same school, and he'd seen her in the hallway. Once or twice she'd smiled at him and lifted her hand toward him as they hurried to their different classrooms.

Billy called the families who lived upstairs "those foreigners" and said that they couldn't even speak English. T.J. knew that wasn't true of Iza, but he never corrected Billy.

Now he wished she would come out. He imagined himself saying hello and her answering, like a friend. Suddenly playing his step game all alone was lame.

He didn't like the way Billy had guessed that he had no friends. T.J. wished he had a gang of boys waiting for him on the sidewalk. He could almost hear them calling his name and begging him to play first baseman in the vacant lot around the corner.

But in his real world, except for school, T.J. hardly ventured outside. Whenever Momma was gone, he stayed in the apartment to keep Angela happy and occupied. He didn't want to leave her alone with Billy, ever.

On the rare occasions when Momma was home without Billy there, T.J. stuck around, mostly watching TV. He wasn't sure why he was almost afraid to leave when Momma was home. Maybe because she might think he didn't care about her if he ran off to play with friends. If Momma thought he didn't care about her, why would she care about him? Or Angela?

Angela. She was getting old enough now to want more

room than their apartment provided. When they first moved here, she'd begun to nag T.J. when Momma was asleep. "Let's go out and play. Come on, T.J. Don't be a 'fraidy-cat," she'd beg.

But so far he'd been able to distract her with television, comics, and food. Now that Billy had moved in, they had a huge TV—not just the old one that didn't work—and both a DVD and a CD player.

Every weekend Billy brought home a gift for Angela. Fancy slippers one week. A gold tiara the next. Then a Barbie doll with all sorts of clothes and accessories.

No wonder Angela was willing to climb on his lap, T.J. thought as he began to move his feet slowly on the steps, then a little faster.

The only present Billy had given T.J. was a football. But Billy never offered to go to the park and play with him. And T.J. never asked because he didn't think Billy would be a very patient coach.

By now T.J. had reached the bottom of the stairs. He started back up, doing the same step game in reverse. Going up and then back down, but making progress toward the top. Faster and faster, his feet making a wild tapping music all their own.

"What are you doing out here?" It was Momma, coming up behind him. He hadn't heard the door to the building open.

"Nothing," he replied, looking down at her as she climbed toward him, her hair a lighter shade of reddish-gold than when she left. Then he said quickly, before he could stop himself, "I don't like Billy. How come you go and leave us with him?"

She was next to him now, and the fresh-flowery scent of her perfume replaced the smell of old food in the air. Momma gave him a sideways hug. "T.J. Please stop worrying. Billy's good to me. That's what matters. And I've told him, 'Love me, love my kids.'"

"Sure, Momma. Like that really works."

"T.J.! You don't know Billy. He's had a hard life. He's gone through a lot. And he's not used to being around kids, let alone living with them. He's doing the best he can. You and Angela need to behave. Then Billy won't be so upset."

T.J. said nothing.

They continued up the steps to the landing. Momma turned to face T.J. "And I need Billy. He's paying all the bills now. He makes me happy. He makes me laugh. And without him, how would I have money to look good? You like my hair this color?" She swung her head from side to side. Shimmering strands of hair moved, catching what little light came from the window at the end of the hallway.

T.J. wanted to say, *You should be happy with just me and Angela.* But instead he stood, silent, and let Momma hug him again and give him a kiss on the forehead.

When they got back inside the apartment, Billy didn't get up from the couch. He was lying down now, his head leaning against the armrest, his baseball cap covering his face. The blue pillow propped up his feet.

Angela was at the table, tearing pages out of T.J.'s comic book.

"What are you doing?" T.J. yelled as he dashed toward her and snatched the remains from her.

"Spider-Man is stupid," Angela said. "I need paper for birds." She collected the pages she'd torn out and held them against her chest. "Mine!" she said, as if she were a baby again instead of a five-year-old.

"No! Give 'em back! I have to tape the book back together."
T.J. tried to pry the pages from Angela's fingers, but he knew
they'd tear if he pulled too hard. "Momma! Make her give
them back to me!"

"Oh, T.J., stop the drama!" Momma glanced anxiously at
Billy. "It's just a comic book."

"What birds?" Billy asked, his voice groggy, as he strug-
gled to a sitting position.

"Birds? What are you talking about?" Momma was
pushing Angela away from the table and toward the bathroom, the only extra room in the apartment.

"*My* birds!" shrieked Angela. She turned from Momma,
still clutching the comic book pages, and dove under the table,
where she scuttled into the center.

"You buy some dammed birds while you were gone, Celia?
This apartment is full enough with these stupid kids in it."
Billy lumbered into the kitchen area and glared at T.J., who
was holding his tattered comic book against his heart. T.J.
wished he were Spider-Man and could climb out a window
and up the side of the building to the roof.

Momma's laugh sounded forced. "No, of course I didn't
buy a bird! I don't know what she's talking about."

T.J. realized Momma wasn't going to be any help. He
clung to his comic book as he ran to the bathroom so Billy
wouldn't see the tears in his eyes.

Later that night, after Momma and Billy had gone to bed,
Angela showed T.J. the reddish purple bruise on her arm.
"He's mean," she whispered. T.J. nodded and tugged more of
the blanket onto his side of the bed.

"Look, T.J." She was still talking softly as she pulled two

paper birds out of the big popcorn can. "I 'membered how to do it. I used Momma's scissors to make the paper square. Then I folded—"

"They're good," T.J. interrupted. By then, he had put what was left of his comic book under the mattress, and his anger had evaporated like the tears on his face.

"I made more." Angela turned the can upside down over the blanket.

T.J. studied the birds in the light from the street lamp outside the window. Seven of them, looking strangely multicolored with comic book images on their wings and heads.

"They can fly away," Angela whispered.

T.J. nodded. He was surprised that Angela remembered what Ray had taught her so long ago. He almost wished he had learned how to make paper birds too.

15

NOW—

"Timothy?"

T.J. shuts his life book and struggles out of his memories to stare at the man standing over him.

It's Dan. His pretend father. That's how T.J. thinks of him sometimes. Even though the adoption was made final two months ago, and Dan is his official father now.

"You were sleeping, T.J." Dan says this gently.

"Was not."

Dan sits down beside T.J. His long legs stretch out across the green linoleum floor. One shoe is untied. As if he can feel T.J.'s gaze, Dan pulls his foot back and carefully, methodically, ties his shoe, giving the laces a yank so hard his chair makes a little jerk.

"How ..." T.J. swallows. "How's Angela?"

Dan sighs. "Not conscious. Not yet. The longer she's unconscious the more serious it could be. But so far the doctors haven't found anything ... anything too terrible. So that's good news. There's a chance—the doctors hope she'll wake up soon. Your mom thought you'd like to know that. About the doctors' hoping."

"My mom?" For just a nanosecond, T.J. is confused. Then he adds quickly, "Oh, yeah, sure."

He expects Dan to get up and go back through the swinging doors, but he stays sitting, the leg with the freshly tied shoe pulled back under his chair.

"Maybe she wants to stay asleep," T.J. says softly. He's

surprised those words came out. He only meant to think them, not say them aloud. Sometimes *he* used to want to stay asleep. Back when Billy was in their lives, and T.J. had trouble facing yet another day of gnawing fear. But not recently.

Now, most days, he likes waking up and having breakfast in the bright kitchen. Marlene sometimes gives him an extra helping of scrambled eggs or another strip of crisp bacon. And homemade biscuits, soggy in the middle with melted butter and sweet with a dollop of strawberry jam. Those breakfasts are mostly on weekends, when Marlene doesn't have to rush off with them to school. During the week they eat cereal, just like in their other life. Marlene is a kindergarten teacher in the same school where Angela is a third grader. She always gives him and Angela money for school lunches. They never have to sign up for free lunch tickets.

Dan looks at T.J. "What did you say?"

"Nothing."

"Okay. I know this is hard for you too." Dan's voice has dropped to a whisper. "But you might feel a little better if you talked to me."

T.J. feels a swift rise of alarm that sets his heart racing. Does Dan know why Angela fell? T.J. sits mutely.

"You're like a hard shell, T.J.," Dan continues. "I wish you'd just open up sometimes about how you're feeling. Just once." By now he seems to be talking to himself.

T.J. takes in a gulp of air. Out of the corner of his eye, he notices that Dan's shirt is rumpled as if he's slept in it, and his hair is messy, a small tuft standing up at the back of his head. Usually Dan is neat as a folded map.

Dan clears his throat. "I just want her to wake up. I want to see her smile."

T.J. can't help wondering if Dan would be that anxious to see *his* smile. Even though Dan never says it, T.J. senses that he's disappointed in his new son.

Or maybe it's T.J. who's disappointed in Dan. Slowly, T.J. turns that idea over in his mind.

Biting one thumbnail, T.J. stares at the floor. Dan is nothing like Ray, the only man Momma loved who seemed to really care about T.J. and Angela. But Ray didn't stick around. His parents showed up and he was out of there.

Dan is the one—and Marlene too—who signed all those papers in front of the judge, making the adoption final. *Adoption Day*, Marlene wrote in bold red letters on the calendar hanging in the kitchen. They took dozens of pictures— of him and Angela, the judge, the social worker, Mrs. Cox, and their new grandparents.

And Marlene has been working on a special Adoption Day scrapbook. They call T.J. "our son" and Angela "our daughter." T.J. has heard them do that when talking to friends and relatives. At home, Dan and Marlene use words like "commitment" and "family." They seem to mean it.

But what do they know? T.J. thinks. Signing a piece of paper is easy. He remembers all those notes that Momma used to write and sign for teachers. Living as a family—being a real family—is not easy.

T.J. is certain, deep down, that Momma loved him and Angela. Yet look what happened. Billy happened and every-thing fell apart.

Fell apart. Fell.

Fell. That one word repeats itself inside T.J.'s head, and he sees Angela falling from the banister. Like one of her stupid paper birds that didn't have the brains to fly.

Angela being unconscious in the Emergency Room is worse than anything that happened before. Worse than the time Momma left them with Tanya or when Ray deserted them. Worse than all the bad times with Billy.

"We have to keep hoping. Right, kiddo?" Dan asks quietly.

T.J. feels tears trying to fill his eyes. "Okay, right," he mumbles. He hasn't cried—not once—since he and Angela moved into Dan and Marlene's two-story suburban house with the yard and the swing and the wading pool.

He's not crying now.

"Don't worry." Dan reaches over and pats T.J. on the shoulder. "We'll get through this. I remember when my brother—you met Uncle Glen at that picnic in July—broke his leg. The whole family was in a panic. It happened when he fell out of a hayloft at our grandparents' farm. The bone was sticking out a little bit, and our mother, she fainted. So we all thought she'd had a heart attack or something."

T.J. swallows, tasting tears. He feels strange. In a way, he likes Dan sitting beside him, telling him not to worry. But a broken leg isn't so bad. Not like falling off a banister and getting knocked out and not waking up for ages. Or never waking up.

T.J. wipes his nose on the sleeve of his shirt.

Dan hops up and walks to the receptionist and returns with a wad of tissues. He sits back down and blows his own nose, then offers a couple of tissues to T.J., who takes them and wipes his whole face, surprised that the tissues are scented. They smell like the lilacs that grew next to the house where Momma's parents lived.

"My brother's leg was in a cast for at least four months," Dan says. "He got so he could race me up and down stairs on his crutches—and win. Always had to win. That's Glen. Very competitive. He recovered completely and ran track in high school. Won lots of ribbons. Trophies too."

Dan glances at T.J. and continues, "Sorry, kiddo, guess you can tell I've always been a bit jealous of Uncle Glen. Remember meeting Josh and Karen and little Michael at the picnic?"

"Uh … maybe."

"They're Glen's kids. You'll see them again at Thanksgiving. They're driving up from Tennessee this year."

"Is Josh that teenager with the shaved head and skull tattoo and the big hoop earrings?"

"Yup. Joshua Andrew." Dan meets T.J.'s gaze and nods just slightly. Then he straightens in his chair and says, "Now, about Angela. The doctors have decided they're going to move her into the Pediatric Intensive Care Unit. So they can monitor her. Watch over her with all those machines. It gives me the creeps, seeing her all hooked up like that."

T.J. shuts his eyes, but he can't block out an image of Angela with wires going into her veins. Probably attached to her head too. He shivers.

"You cold?" asks Dan. "You should get up and walk around. What'd you have to eat?"

T.J. shrugs. "I'm not hungry."

Dan frowns, looking concerned. "You need to eat, T.J. You want to come with me to the hospital cafeteria? I saw a sign for it over there. I bet they've got some good macaroni and cheese. You like that, right?"

T.J. shakes his head. "No," he says firmly.

Dan sighs. "Okay. I'm going back. Angela might be moved by now. I'll check and see if kids are allowed to visit in the PIC Unit."

"I'm twelve," T.J. reminds him. Dan is already leaving,

but he turns to wave one hand at T.J. before he goes through the swinging doors.

With Dan gone, T.J. feels a mixture of regret and relief. Standing up, he digs some coins out of his pocket and stares at them. There's a metallic taste in his mouth. He jiggles the coins in his hand, listening to the tiny sound of them clicking together. None of the other people in the waiting room look at him. He glances down at the cover of his life book on the chair seat and then walks away, wondering if anyone will steal it before he gets back from the vending machines around the corner.

The photo album is lying open when T.J. returns to the waiting room. He holds a candy bar half-eaten in his hand. He peers around the room accusingly, but no one looks guilty of having turned to the page with the picture that stares up at him. It's the one of Billy, with the angry red marks coming out of his head. With a shiver, T.J. remembers when Billy almost looked like that, his face so flushed with anger he seemed to give off visible sparks and streaks of fury.

T.J. shuts the book with a slap and plops into the seat beside it. He eats the candy bar in tiny nibbles, savoring the sweetness and the crunch of nuts. He tries to make his mind blank, but the picture he made of Billy over a year ago seems imprinted on his brain. Like when you stare at a lamp and then look away with your eyes shut, but you can still see the image.

He crumples the candy wrapper and looks for a trash can but doesn't see one. He shoves the wrapper in his pocket and leans back, stretching out his legs. Funny, just like Dan—one of his sneakers is untied. T.J. stares at the shoelace and realizes that the bow is undone, but the lace has a knot in it. He sits still and deliberately ignores his untied shoe.

16

After Angela made that first paper bird on her own, there was no stopping her. To save T.J.'s comic books, their mother bought a thick pack of computer paper and left it on the kitchen counter amid the other items that collected there: pens and pencils, scribbled notes on scraps of paper, boxes half full of cereal, empty pizza containers, cups of coffee that were cold and covered with a scummy film.

"Why don't you clean up this pig pen?" Billy asked Momma when he came home.

"I'm tired. I take care of the kids all day long."

Billy waved his long arms. "They're in school! I'm beginning to think you're just lazy."

"Angela is only in kindergarten. She's home half the day, getting into stuff, making one mess after another. Do you want to put her back in daycare? Then I'd have time to clean and cook."

"Daycare? Waste of money." Billy plopped onto the couch, and T.J. moved quickly onto the floor.

Momma was still talking. "*You* go wherever you want. We need to get out more. Together, Billy. I need a break."

Billy reached for Momma and gave her a kiss on the lips. He noticed T.J. watching from his spot on the floor in front of the TV. Billy said, winking at Momma, "Look at that kid. All eyes. You want to learn how to kiss, kid? Watch your new daddy."

He pulled Momma toward him with his huge, hairy hands and kissed her again for so long that T.J. felt his own lungs would burst as he held his breath. Momma staggered away, laughing, when Billy let her go.

"That's how it's done, wimp. Or should I say wimpette? Maybe you'll be kissing your own kind when you grow up."

T.J.'s eyes were stinging, and his hands had clenched into knots on their own. But by now Billy was no longer interested in him.

Billy addressed Momma, his voice soft now. "I've been working on a big deal. Real big. I'm getting rid of all this small stuff." He gestured toward several boxes sitting near the door. "We'll have plenty of time and money soon, Celia."

Angela, who had scurried under the table when Billy came through the apartment door, now came crawling out. She made T.J. think of a stray cat he'd seen the other day, lurking and skulking away when he tried to call it over.

Without quite standing up, Angela reached for a sheet of paper, yanking it out from under a can of pop. She was back under the table even as the can fell. T.J. watched, unable to react quickly enough, as the can smacked the floor and a puddle of liquid spread toward Billy, who lifted his feet out of the way. "Damn kids! Look at this mess! It's running under the couch. Get a rag and clean it up!" he bellowed at T.J.

T.J. said, "I didn't do it. She did." He pointed toward the table.

"I told *you* to clean it up. When I tell you to move, *move*!"

T.J. started toward the kitchen sink for a towel, but he had to get around Billy. As he ran past, Billy kicked at his legs, and the hard toe of his shoe connected with the side of T.J.'s left knee.

T.J. stumbled forward, hitting his forehead on the edge of the counter and then crashing to the floor.

The pain in his left knee squeezed out all thoughts as he curled into a ball, hugging his body with his elbows, afraid to move for fear his leg would fall apart.

Momma screamed. "He's bleeding!"

Blood dripped onto his jeans and blurred his vision. He reached up and felt the gash high on his forehead.

"Shit!" Billy was there, pressing a towel against the cut, holding T.J. steady. "Keep still."

The heavy, sick odor of Billy's breath combined with the pain in T.J.'s knee made his stomach heave. He swallowed.

Billy said, "Hold still. We have to make this bleeding stop."

T.J. shivered and his teeth began to chatter. He could feel the rough hair on Billy's arm against his neck, the towel on his forehead. His mother was standing nearby, Angela clinging to her legs.

"Billy! Look at all that blood!" Momma said. "He needs to get that sewn up at the hospital."

"He's fine! You want some smart-ass doctor wondering how he did it? You want them all over us, asking questions? They never trust people like us, Celia."

"It was an *accident*, Billy. He needs help!"

"You're the one has the kids. Not me. You want to take him to the ER, go right ahead. I'll be gone, totally *gone*, when you get back. Besides, I bet Terry Jerry doesn't want to go to any hospital. Do you?"

By then T.J. could feel the pain in his head. But it was the throbbing knee that made him want to stay still. He didn't dare open his mouth. The only sound that would come out was a scream.

Billy was talking into his face. "They'll tie you down and

sew you up with a gigantic needle and thick thread. You'll look like Frankenstein when they get done with you. So, do you want your mother to take you? Do you?"

"No," whispered T.J.

"What? I can't hear you!"

"No. No. No," T.J. said, and he felt a sharp pain in his head with each word.

He missed a week of school. Long enough for the wound on his head to stop oozing blood. He hadn't had his hair trimmed for a while, so it hung down over his forehead and covered the injury. Every day that week, Momma removed the old bandage, treated the cut with an antibiotic ointment she'd bought at a drugstore, and pressed a new bandage in place.

T.J. was almost glad he'd gotten hurt because Momma spent time with him, smoothing the ointment on his forehead, talking to him in short, cheerful sentences. She told him Billy was sorry about the accident. T.J. told her his knee hurt lots worse than his head, and she found an elastic bandage and wrapped his knee, so he was able to walk with only a slight limp.

Billy watched T.J. move awkwardly around the apartment but said nothing. Maybe being visibly injured was a good thing in some ways, T.J. thought. He now had a brief hold over Billy. He was almost certain that Billy wouldn't grab him or push him around while he was limping. And he was thankful for Billy's silence, which seemed like a small piece of quiet.

T.J.'s fourth-grade teacher was nothing like Mrs. Herman from the year before. Miss Snicket had trouble controlling the class. Someone was always yelling or throwing a pencil or whacking another kid. So T.J.'s cut forehead and limp were never mentioned, never noticed.

And he wasn't even sure Miss Snicket had been aware of his empty seat for a week. When he came back, she looked at him just briefly, gave a strained smile, and said vaguely, "Oh, there you are." She never requested his missing homework or asked him why he'd been gone, but Momma had written a note on pretty paper with flowers that explained all about the accident. Not the real accident, but the pretend one that had happened when T.J. was carrying groceries up the stairs and slipped and fell, cutting his head and hurting his knee.

"Nothing serious, you understand, but the doctor felt it best that he be kept quiet and at home for a week."

17

It was late one night when T.J. heard more about the big deal that Billy had mentioned to Momma. Over the past few weeks, all the stolen stuff had disappeared and no new boxes had arrived.

T.J., Angela, and Momma were watching the new TV that Billy had provided to replace Momma's broken one. They sprawled on her bed, clutching pillows and shoving bare feet under a twisted blanket. Billy was talking on his cell phone out in the living room.

"Don't bug him, you two," Momma said. "He's got important business to take care of."

T.J. wrinkled his nose. The bed smelled more like Billy than Momma.

"I love this one," Angela said as an ad for cat food came on the TV. It featured a talking and singing cat. T.J. thought it looked way too fake, the way the cat's mouth moved to form human words. But Angela began bouncing on the bed and singing along with the cat.

"I gotta go pee," T.J. mumbled.

He wondered if he could sneak out into Billy territory and watch whatever was on the other TV.

"Come right back in here when you're done," Momma said, as if she'd read his mind.

T.J. sighed. The bathroom was located off the hallway close to the living room. His bare feet were silent, and the hallway was dark. Just before turning into the bathroom, T.J.

stopped. The only light in the living room was coming from the TV, which was turned down so low that Billy's voice intermingled with those of the actors on the cop show.

T.J. slowed his breathing and rested his right foot on top of his left. He listened.

He always listened. Sometimes he heard Billy and Momma talking or arguing. Lots of times Billy was on the phone, "making contacts," as he told Momma. Or Billy would have friends over, and they'd be drinking and talking. Mostly Billy would be talking garbage, just rambling on about things he'd done or telling stupid jokes that made no sense to T.J., and even when they did, he thought they weren't funny. At all.

But this night, Billy's voice sounded different. There was a note of tension in it. Or maybe excitement. T.J. did need to pee, but he stayed where he'd stopped.

Billy was talking quietly but still loud enough for T.J. to hear if he concentrated and remained totally still.

"I know. I hear what you're sayin'. But this'll be a big deal—worth the risk," Billy said just as the TV music began to sound frantic. "Nah. No one'll suspect. It's been over three years since Tammy worked for them … No. She moved to California … Yeah, I checked. The kid will fit."

T.J.'s mouth felt dry, and he moved his tongue back and forth against his teeth as he tried to understand what Billy meant. A commercial for some sort of medication came on at a higher volume. T.J. felt a moment of frustration. Then Billy muted the TV.

Silence.

T.J. tried not to take a breath.

"No problem," said Billy. "Yeah … I meant the girl … Yeah. I checked that too. You think I'm an idiot?"

Silence.

"Nah, not that one. The one in the bathroom by that closet."

T.J. knew there was a small linen closet built into the wall, right there, next to him in the dark. He felt goose bumps rising on his arms.

More silence, then the thin, distant wail of a real police siren.

"I'm gonna tell her to take the night off ... Nah, not out of town. She'll go to some bar and have a blast ... You kidding? She hasn't worked since I moved in. She'll be like a cat let out of a bag, getting to go out all night ... Sure. She trusts me with the kids. I'm their daddy now."

Billy listened for a few moments, then laughed so hard he began to cough. When he recovered, he said, "Just you and me on this one ... Right, fifty-fifty. I got a buyer all lined up. Not to worry ... Right, two-thirty." The sound on the TV came back on.

T.J. scuttled back to Momma's bedroom. He'd pee later. Momma and Angela were both asleep on the bed.

That night and for the next few nights, T.J. tried to be awake at 2 a.m. He managed to wake up at 1:30 the first night, but the door to the bedroom where Momma and Billy slept was shut, and he could hear Billy's snoring. He slept through the second night and woke at 4:30 on the third.

Feeling groggy, he stared at the clock on the wall in the kitchen. It gave off a faint light, which, combined with the street lamp, illuminated the living room enough so he could see immediately that Angela was not on her side of the fold-out couch. Even so, he reached over, pressing his hands into the blankets, searching for her curled body. He looked toward the bathroom door, but it was partway open, no light on. Empty.

T.J.'s breath came in small, ragged gasps as he got up and made his way down the short hallway to Momma's bedroom. The bed was empty.

He had no clue where they'd gone, and his mind seemed to be working in slow motion.

T.J. couldn't remember a time when he had been left totally alone. Without Angela.

He lay back down on his side of the couch but averted his eyes from the empty spot that should have contained Angela. T.J. flipped the blankets, trying to cover his chilled toes. When he leaned his head on the armrest, he felt the scratch of the upholstery fabric and smelled the scent of cigarettes.

T.J. didn't want Billy to come back and find him awake, so he lay still, pretending to be asleep.

Light was flooding the room when T.J. opened his eyes. He blinked a couple of times, trying to get fully awake. The TV was on, and he realized it was Saturday morning cartoon time. Angela was already sitting up on the bed, watching TV and eating sugar-coated generic cereal out of the box.

"Where's Momma?" he asked.

"Bedroom, sleeping," Angela said, crunching loudly as she talked.

"And Billy?"

"Him, too."

T.J. wasn't sure which question to ask next. He had so many. "You sure they're asleep?"

Angela nodded. "Momma's sick. She threw up on the stairs when they came home. She said it was Billy's fault 'cause he left her at that bar and she didn't have enough money for a cab. He said that was her fault for spending it all on beer. She said he shouldn't have dropped her off at a bar that was so far away and then not come back until dawn. He said that he thought she'd be thrilled to be so far away from her bratty kids. She said he—" Angela stopped to breathe.

T.J. stared at his sister. He'd seen Momma take a pill sometimes to stay awake for work, and he suspected that Billy had given Angela something like that. Her voice was too high and excited, and he'd never heard her talk so fast or say so much at once.

"She said he should shut his trap," Angela went on. "And he quit talking, and Momma came over and kissed me and then you. I pretended to be asleep. Then they went to bed. I pretended, but you were asleep for real."

This wasn't making a lot of sense to T.J. even when he tried to combine it with what he'd heard Billy say on the phone.

Angela took another fistful of cereal. T.J. waited.

Turning her bright gaze on him, Angela said, "And you didn't wake up before, when Billy came for me. He said you'd told him to let you sleep. That you didn't want to come with us. Why didn't you want to come? I was scaredified."

"I'm sorry, Angela. I tried to stay awake." T.J. wondered if Billy had given him a sleeping pill in last night's food. "Where did you go? With Billy."

"I'm not supposed to tell." She pulled her legs back and folded them under the blanket, as if withdrawing into a secret position. T.J. noticed she was wearing a black leotard and black tights.

"Did Billy give you that dance outfit?"

Angela looked at him sideways. "Yeah."

"You can tell me where you went. I can keep a secret."

Angela stuck out her lower lip. "No."

"Did Momma go too?"

"I already told you. Billy took Momma to that bar. Before he woke me up and gave me the dance stuff. He said he would take me to a party. That's why I needed the dance stuff. I was going to dance. But I wanted you to come." Angela pulled another fistful of cereal out of the box and jammed it into her mouth.

T.J. noticed dark smudges under her eyes that reminded him of the way Momma looked with runny mascara after she'd been crying.

"Did you dance?" he asked softly.

"No." Angela rubbed her eyes with the backs of both hands. The cereal box tipped and almost landed on the floor. "He said he'd buy me a pony. Or anything I wanted. I said I wanted a bird. I'm getting a parakeet." She looked at T.J. with her head tilted back, as if to challenge him to contradict her.

"Billy is going to buy you a parakeet?"

"Yeah. A real, alive parakeet. I wanted it right now. But Billy said I could wear this till I get my parakeet. Then I have to give it back. So Billy can sell it to some guy who's out of town right now." Angela reached down into the front of her leotard and pulled out a chain with a pendant on the end. "See? Billy says it's real gold. And those sparkly bits? Real diamonds."

Gold and diamonds! Angela wouldn't know or care about whether some dumb necklace was real or fake. All of which made T.J. think it was true.

T.J. shivered. "Billy trusts you with a necklace like that? Why?"

Angela cocked her head to one side and blinked. "Because I did everything right. He said I should wear it under my shirt and not tell anybody where I really got it. Not Momma or you or any of his friends—especially his friend that drove us. If I tell, he won't get me my parakeet." She slipped the necklace back inside her leotard. "He said if anybody saw it, I should say that my boyfriend at school gave it to me. I told him I have three boyfriends and which one gave it to me? But Billy said not to worry. Billy's proud of me, and he said I didn't have to dance. But I wanted to dance."

T.J.'s head was beginning to ache. "Where were you when you didn't have to dance?"

She looked at him slyly. "I promised not to tell. You guess."

T.J. guessed a TV station, a grocery store, an airport, a pet shop, a bus station, and a warehouse. Angela said no to all until the warehouse.

"What's that? A warehouse?"

"It's like a big, plain building. With stuff stored inside it."

She shook her head. "No. This was fancy. A real fancy place with trees around it and bushes and real tall windows. The prettiest house. Like a fairytale castle—almost. "

"A house," T.J. whispered. "So did you visit Billy's friends at that house?"

"No. Nobody was home." Angela shoved the cereal box onto the floor and began twisting a lock of hair around her finger. She looked as if she would pop her thumb in her mouth at any moment. Then she'd quit talking.

"Nobody was home?" T.J. repeated with an encouraging nod.

"Nope. But one of his friends went with us. He drove the van."

"So, did you and Billy and Billy's friend go into the fancy house?"

"*I* went in. Billy said I was just the right size. That you were too big and a wuss. They had a ladder and put me through a teeny-tiny window in a bathroom. I had my own flashlight. I went to the right."

Angela held up her two hands. A blue X had been drawn on her right palm. "I know which is right, but Billy said the X would keep me from getting mixed up. If I went the wrong way, I might open a door with an alarm. And the cops would come."

T.J. nodded. Now that she was talking, he didn't want to say anything that would make her stop.

"I went right into a hallway and down eleven steps and opened a door. It had a lock … a sort of sliding lock on it. But Billy showed me how to open it. He had a lock just like it in the van, and I practiced. When I unlocked the door, Billy and his friend came in. I had to sit by the door and not make a sound. I was all alone. It smelled funny. Billy and his friend got stuff from the house and went out the door. Then I had to lock the door again and go back and climb out the window. I was afraid. I thought they would leave me there. Why didn't you want to come, T.J.? I was so scaredified."

"I'm sorry. I was asleep. Billy lied to you, Angela. I never told him not to wake me. If I'd been awake, I would have made him leave you home. With me."

Angela stared at him, then blinked rapidly. "If Billy wanted you to come, he would *make* you come. But he wanted me. Just me." Angela eyes looked wet, but she wasn't crying. "I wanted to dance. I was afraid. But I get to wear this necklace till I get my *real,* green parakeet."

"Yeah. We'll see. A green parakeet."

"He promised," Angela said fiercely.

18

T.J. knew he had to tell Momma what Billy had done. But as the days slunk past, it got harder to bring it up. Especially since Momma seemed so happy. Billy bought her a whole bunch of new clothes that she modeled for T.J. and Angela when they got home from school. Even new shoes and purses with shiny buckles. And there was talk of a trip to Las Vegas.

"We'll go after school lets out for the summer," Momma told them about a week after the robbery. Billy had already gone into the bedroom, and T.J. could hear the muttering sounds of TV voices through the closed door. Momma was yanking the couch out to turn it into a bed. Usually that was T.J.'s job, but tonight Momma was full of energy and smiles. "It'll be a real family vacation."

"What about my parakeet?" asked Angela.

"Parakeet? Is that what you're calling them now?" Momma asked. "Which one, honey? You've got a whole gigantic tin can full of those paper birds." Momma smiled and ran her fingers through Angela's long hair.

"Ouch! Stop!" Angela winced and jumped away. "I want my real, green parakeet. I want it now. He promised!"

"Who promised? What's she talking about, T.J.?"

It was the perfect opening. Now he could tell Momma what sort of person Billy really was. But T.J. felt his throat tightening. He glanced at Angela, who had climbed up onto the fold-out couch and was standing there with her hands planted on her hips.

Before T.J. could begin to answer, Angela said, "Billy. He promised to buy me a real, alive parakeet. I don't want to go to Las Vegas. I want my parakeet!" Her voice rose to a familiar pitch. It had been many months since Angela had had a tantrum, but T.J. could hear one coming now.

"Why would Billy buy you a parakeet, Angela?" Momma was shaking her head.

"I want my bird!" Angela flung herself face down on the couch and began to scream. "Parakeet! Keet! Keet! Keet!" It was a high-pitched, birdlike noise that made T.J.'s teeth ache.

"Angela! Shut up!" Momma yelled. "What's gotten into you? T.J., what's this all about?"

Angela stopped screeching abruptly and sat up and cried, "Billy promised! Ask him!" She leaped off the couch and grabbed her mother's hand and dragged her toward the bedroom.

Stop! T.J. screamed silently. But it was too late.

Billy flung open the door and stomped into the hallway. "I can't hear myself think! What's she caterwauling about?"

"My parakeet!" Angela was still clinging to Momma's hand, but she had slipped back so that she was partially shielded by their mother's body.

Billy shook his head. "You got to wear that special necklace, remember?"

Angela said loudly, "You made me give it back to you yesterday. But you didn't give me my parakeet."

"So?" Billy shrugged. "Celia, just shut her up. I have a headache."

"I saw where you hid it," Angela said. "In a tiny box in your boot."

"What?" Billy's eyes turned into slits of darkness.

"I took it," said Angela.

"The buyer's expecting it tonight. Angela! Where's that necklace? Give it to me now!"

"Where's my parakeet!" Angela stepped away from Momma, then reached inside her shirt and pulled out the necklace.

"You little thief!" Billy glared at Angela. "I'll teach you not to get into my things!"

T.J. was sure that Angela finally realized Billy's promise had been a lie.

"Angela!" Momma said as she tried to turn and grab Angela's arm. "You told me Jamel—or was it Daniel?—gave that to you at school."

Ignoring Momma, Angela taunted Billy. "I don't even like this old, dumb necklace!" She pulled it forward and gave it sharp yanks as she said, "I. Hate. It! I. Hate. It!"

Billy's voice became more menacing. "Stop, Angela! You'll break it!"

"I. Hate. It! I. Hate. It!" Angela ran through the living room and circled the couch, still giving the necklace sharp jerks.

Momma was frowning and looking at T.J., but he avoided meeting her eyes.

"Give me that necklace!" Billy roared. "That's real gold! Real diamonds!"

"You gimme my parakeet and I'll give you back this ugly ol' necklace!" Angela leaped onto the couch and began to bounce. The necklace flapped against her thin chest.

"Stop that!" yelled Billy.

Angela clapped her hands over her ears and kept bouncing. "I can't hear you!" she said in a singsong voice.

"You little—" Billy lunged at Angela, but she was too quick. She was off the couch and dashing behind Momma and T.J. with Billy tripping over couch cushions as he tried to catch her. Angela slipped the necklace over her head as she ran.

T.J. felt a wave of relief. He thought she was going to throw the necklace at Billy. But Angela kept it clutched in her hand and headed for the bathroom.

She was so little and so quick!

She shut the bathroom door, which slowed Billy's awkward dash to catch her. T.J. heard the toilet flush as Billy flung open the door and lunged after her.

Angela's scream came before the sound of the flush was complete. T.J. pressed his hands over his ears and stepped backwards.

Billy called Angela a bunch of filthy names, then screamed, "Shut up! Shut up!"

T.J. was sure the necklace was gone.

Momma pushed past T.J. and tried to peer into the bathroom, but Billy slammed the door in her face.

Angela's wordless cries grew louder. Then abruptly stopped.

Through the closed door T.J. could hear wild splashing and gurgling sounds.

A short scream. More gurgling.

"Billy? What's going on?" Momma yelled, but she didn't attempt to open the bathroom door.

T.J. knew what Billy was doing. And he thought Momma knew too.

The toilet flushed again. Strangled screams. Cut off.

Turning away, T.J. found the door to the apartment hallway right there within two steps. *Escape!*

As he ran out into the dimly lit hallway he heard their mother's voice, raised to a terrified screech. "Billy! Stop!"

The apartment door closed behind T.J., but he didn't even worry about having a key. He ran up to the third floor. One of these doors belonged to the girl's family, but he didn't know which. He knocked on the first one he reached.

Hard. Again and again. No answer.

Dashing to the next apartment, he could hear someone's muffled wailing from below.

He'd barely started to pound on the door when it opened. T.J. gulped and looked up at the dark man standing in front of him.

"Help," he whispered.

The man frowned and shook his head.

Then the girl appeared beside her father, feet bare and hair hanging loose. Her eyes met T.J.'s for a moment, and he licked his lips and said, "Please, help us."

"T.J.? T.J.!" It was Billy's jackhammer voice coming from the stairway. "Where are you?"

The man heard Billy too and quickly shut the door, leaving T.J. alone in the hallway.

He stood still. If he knocked on another door, Billy would hear him. He tried to silence his jagged breathing.

Then he heard Billy's feet pounding toward the street-level entryway.

Leaning his back against the hallway wall, T.J. felt the bones of his spine, cold through his thin shirt. He listened to the quiet.

T.J. tried to keep his mind blank as he waited. But he couldn't control a mess of scary, confusing thoughts. Billy might come back and search the stairway and hallways. Or he might be gone for the night. If Billy hurt Angela really bad, maybe he'd never come back. T.J. took a deep breath, and then he ran quickly and quietly to the second floor.

The door to their apartment was shut, and he tapped lightly.

"T.J.!" Momma flung open the door and pulled him to her. "Where have you been? Billy went to look for you."

He pushed away the warmth and comfort of his mother's arms, shut the door, then locked it and hooked the chain.

When he turned around, he heard Angela. He felt an intense rush of relief. Peering over the back of the couch, he saw her huddled in a blanket, sobbing, with her thumb in her mouth.

"Momma," T.J. said. "Did Billy take his key?"

"I don't know. What are you doing? Trying to lock him out?"

"Yes." T.J. pressed his back against the closed door and wished it were covered with Spider-Man's web. Something indestructible.

Momma sat on the edge of the couch. "Billy was really upset with Angela."

T.J.'s mouth was dry. "Momma, we can't let him come back."

Angela's sobs got louder. She scrambled onto her knees and looked at T.J. The front of her T-shirt was soaked, and strands of wet hair clung to her face and dripped onto the blanket.

"Oh, baby," Momma said, waving her hand at Angela. "Please stop that noise. I'm exhausted. I'm going to have a cup of decaf and go to bed."

"We can't let Billy in!" T.J. was not going to let it slide.

"Oh, don't be so melodramatic," Momma said. She got up and went to the closet for a towel and tossed it to Angela. "Dry your hair, Punkin."

Next Momma put a kettle of water on the stove. "If Billy can forgive Angela for throwing away a thousand-dollar necklace, I can forgive him for losing his temper. It won't happen again."

T.J. rubbed his stinging eyes with his fingers. Then he stared at their mother. She'd picked up a sponge and started wiping the countertop.

"Momma, Billy—"

His mother interrupted. "Billy spanked her, is all. Because she did something naughty. He's right, you know. Kids need discipline."

T.J. didn't know what to say. He was sure Momma knew that Billy had done more than give Angela a spanking.

"You're being silly, T.J.," Momma continued. "Angela is just fine. Of course he can come back. I need Billy. He pays the bills, and he's like a daddy to you kids."

T.J. took a deep breath. "He's a no-good daddy."

Angela made a strange moaning sound. He looked at her. She opened her mouth, but didn't say a word. Her wet eyes stared at him and held him still.

Angela shook her head sharply and emphatically. Suddenly T.J. felt uncertain.

A loud, determined knocking at the apartment door startled him.

No one moved. Then the teakettle's thin whistle filled the air, and Momma turned off the burner.

19

"Police! Open the door!"

It was just like a TV show, thought T.J., but his reaction was way different. Now all the saliva in his mouth turned to dust, and his heart did backflips.

Momma shook her head, pointed at him and Angela, and then pressed her finger against her lips before opening the door.

There were two of them, a man and a woman, in uniforms with guns and other equipment strapped to their belts. Momma started talking before they had a chance to ask any questions.

"I'm so sorry, officers. We got kind of loud. Probably some neighbor called in to complain. It won't happen again. I promise." Momma was smiling and looking up at the man cop.

"It's just you and the two kids here, ma'am?"

"That's right." Momma nodded vigorously.

"We had a call about a domestic dispute. With a *man* involved." The woman cop looked younger than Momma. Her dark hair was pulled into a short ponytail that stuck out from under the back of her hat. There was something in her voice that made T.J. realize that she didn't believe what their mother had said.

"Oh, well …" Momma backed up toward the kitchen. "I've got hot water for instant coffee. Would you two like some?"

"No thank you. Please sit down, ma'am, and answer our questions."

The couch was still in bed mode, so Momma and the two police officers sat at the table while T.J. and Angela perched on the edge of the bed. The air felt thick, and T.J. had to breathe slowly to keep from choking.

The interview went on and on. Momma eventually told them about Billy and that he'd spanked Angela. The woman officer turned to Angela with a few questions, but Angela only sucked her thumb and shook her head in answer. When asked about her wet hair, Angela rubbed it with the towel and muttered the word "shower." Her expression was as blank as that of her paper birds. She was acting retarded, T.J. thought.

But Momma told the police officers about the necklace and how it was worth a lot of money.

"So, this Billy Peterson bought this necklace for your daughter?" the man cop asked.

"No. No, he didn't buy it. That necklace was mine for years. My grandmother gave it to me back when I graduated high school."

T.J. felt sweat pooling under his arms and in the palms of his hands, inside his fists. He tried to think what he would say if they asked him what had happened.

He was relieved when one of the officers' radios crackled. As abruptly as they'd arrived, they were gone, called away to another problem somewhere nearby.

After they left, Momma's smile looked too large and pasted on. "See now? Nothing to worry about. Did you hear that dispatcher on the radio? Sounded like a shooting. Our little family dispute is nothing. You remember that, kids. This whole thing was *nothing* at all. And when Billy comes home, you be nice. I can't afford to have you two drive him away."

"I hope he never, ever comes back," said T.J.

"You watch what you say, young man," said Momma. Her eyes were bright as she looked at him, but he could see fear in them. T.J. swallowed the words he wanted to say.

He knew that although his mother might be afraid of Billy, she was even more afraid of his not coming back.

T.J. had trouble sleeping that night. His eyes kept seeking the kitchen wall clock as the minutes ticked by. He tried not to look, hoping that would make the darkness disappear and day come more quickly. Angela murmured in her sleep, then rolled over and flung one hand on top of the blanket. He could hear a faint slurping sound and knew she was sucking the thumb of her other hand.

His eyes strayed to the clock. It was almost 4:00 a.m.

A few minutes later he heard a thump in the hallway. Instantly, his whole body was on alert. After Momma had gone to bed, he had checked the door, and, as he'd expected, she had unchained it. So T.J. had rehooked it. Now he heard more quiet noises and the dull clank of the edge of the opened door as it hit the chain.

Billy muttered a few swear words.

T.J. heard Momma's cell phone ringing, and he knew Billy was calling her. There had been no way of locking Billy out. Momma came rushing from the bedroom and let him in.

"I'm sorry," she whispered. "I must have hooked that dumb chain out of habit."

T.J. lay as still as he could on the couch. He kept his head turned away, his eyes shut, but his ears told him what was happening. Billy had a friend with him, and together the two men carried away Billy's belongings.

Momma was pleading with Billy. "You don't have to move out, really …"

"Yeah, well, I do, Celia. There's no way this can work. You and me? Fine and dandy. You, me, and two brats? No way."

"What about Las Vegas? You promised we'd go together." Momma sounded like Angela, begging to go to Dairy Queen.

"Celia, let me get this stuff outta here. I'll call you."

"You promise? You won't go and forget to call, will you?" Momma's tone was teasing now, but T.J. could detect an undertone of desperation.

"I keep my promises. You know that."

T.J. knew Angela would have challenged Billy on that statement if she'd been awake.

Shortly after Billy and his friend grunted their way out the door with the last of his stuff, T.J. finally relaxed and fell asleep.

By the time the morning light was creeping in the windows, the apartment had lost all signs of Billy. But there was still a reminder in their mother's pinched expression and nervous voice.

"You better hurry, T.J., or you'll miss the bus." They'd all overslept, and he had no desire to get ready and go to school, but it was better than staying with Momma. Her face was blotchy and her eyes rimmed with red. She hadn't bothered to brush her hair. When she got close to him, he could smell her stale breath.

So he went to school, and that afternoon he rode the bus home with Angela, just as if it were a normal day.

Angela said nothing as they walked the short stretch of sidewalk from the school bus stop to their building. Her hair was tangled, and although the early spring day's temperature felt near freezing, she was wearing her pink sweater with no coat.

"Billy won't come back," he told her as they stepped into the entryway. Angela didn't respond. She ran up the stairs, her backpack bouncing against her thin shoulder blades. T.J. didn't know why he felt so apprehensive as he followed her. He was sure he'd spoken the truth. Billy would not return. He'd made a lot of money on that house robbery, and he'd removed all his other stuff, so he had no reason to come back.

But when they reached the apartment door, he and Angela hesitated. Voices were coming from inside. Their mother was talking to a man.

T.J. used his key. The moment they stepped inside, their mother enveloped them in her arms and half hugged, half tugged them toward the table, all the while talking in a quick, loud voice.

"Here they are! You can ask them yourselves now. They know my boyfriend has dumped me and moved out."

T.J. guessed immediately that the two people sitting at the table were investigators from that agency called AFCS for short. He stared at them, a man and a woman.

It was like a replay of the night before with the questions, although some of Momma's answers were different. She probably couldn't remember which lie was which. The woman social worker took him into the bedroom to talk, but he was careful to keep his answers short. Mostly he just shrugged or said he didn't know or didn't remember.

After the interview, the woman gave him a tiny card, a business card, with her name and a phone number. T.J. took it without saying thank you and, later, when the AFCS workers were gone, he crumpled it up and shoved it into the back pocket of his jeans.

20

The next day was Friday. T.J. went to school with a knot of pain in his stomach that no amount of tepid water from the hallway fountain could dissolve or dislodge. All day his mind replayed the visits from the cops and the social workers.

The woman social worker had talked to Angela alone too but T.J. knew his little sister was as adept as Momma at avoiding the truth. He'd noticed the look on the social worker's face when she had returned to the table with Angela, who was sucking her thumb and carrying a purple paper crane in her other hand. Angela's eyes had looked dull and then wary as she glanced at T.J.

After what seemed like hours of questions and hardly any answers, it was just the fact that Billy was gone that had made all the difference. The AFCS worker had told Momma, "Since there's no imminent danger to the children, we have no reason to take them into protective custody. But we will be checking back with you to make sure all's well. That Mr. Peterson sounds like bad news. Do not let him return, Ms. Riley, or you can expect to have these kids back in foster care. That man stays out of your life!"

No matter how many times T.J. remembered those words, he was not reassured. The day felt endless and dreary like the dark spring sky. On the bus ride home, he wanted to sit with Angela, but by the time the fourth graders climbed on Bus #7, his sister was already packed into a seat between two other kindergartners, a small girl with a red hat and another little girl with dark, curly hair. The dark-haired one reminded him of the upstairs girl.

He found a seat with a fourth-grade boy—not a friend, but not an enemy or tormentor either. T.J. tried to make his mind blank. But Billy kept tromping through his brain, taking over his thoughts the way he'd taken over their lives. *He's gone*, T.J. reminded himself. There was no reason to feel so anxious about going home today. Billy was gone for good.

Terrified Jerrified, he thought. That's what Billy would call him back then, when Billy spent hours lurking in the apartment like some predator in its den, gnawing on its victims.

"He's gone," T.J. whispered, and the kid next to him looked over but didn't ask him to repeat his comment.

Totally Junk. Turkey Jerky. Toady Jody. Names Billy had called him jounced in his head as the school bus bumped over the potholed street. With Billy gone those names could be forgotten. Now he was just T.J.

He heard a squeal of laughter and turned his head in time to see Angela releasing one of her paper birds through the narrow opening at the top of the window. The driver glanced in his rear-view mirror and bellowed, "Windows shut!"

T.J. took a deep breath of the damp air as he stepped off the bus after it pulled up and stopped outside their apartment building. He noticed as soon as he and Angela started up the sidewalk that the space allotted to Momma's car was empty.

The door to the apartment was locked, and he had to dig his key out from under his jacket and shirt and undershirt. Angela was dancing beside him. "Hurry up, T.J.! I gotta go pee!"

As soon as he got the door open, Angela dashed past him and into the bathroom. T.J. sensed an extra emptiness to the apartment. The couch cushions were neatly arranged, the blue pillow at one end. Draped over the back was an afghan that Momma sometimes claimed had been crocheted by their grandmother. All six chairs were pushed up to the table in the dining area. No dirty dishes were on the table or countertops. The pile of junk mail was gone.

A piece of white paper leaned against the toaster, and a cell phone sat just in front of the paper to keep it from sliding down. T.J. could see that it was a note, but he waited to go close enough to read it until Angela was done in the bathroom and was trotting past him, heading for the refrigerator.

"I'm starving!"

"Wait, Angela. Momma left us a note."

"What's it say?" Angela was peering into the fridge now and exclaimed, "Wow! Look at all this food! I'm gonna make a sandwich. You want cheese, T.J.?"

T.J. picked up the note. Momma had printed it. As if he were a little kid who couldn't read cursive. Or maybe she thought Angela could read already. Momma might not realize that even though Angela could identify numbers and letters, both upper and lower case, she couldn't actually read yet. But Momma's note was like a first-grade teacher's careful printing, the letters all straight and the curves round and smooth.

"Listen, Angela." He read the note aloud slowly as if he were writing it himself.

Dear T.J. and Angela,
    I've gone to Las Vegas with Billy. Just for the weekend. One last fling, I guess. I went shopping, so there's a ton of food. I've left my cell phone. Just scroll down for Billy's number and press "send." Be sure to go to school on Monday, and when

you get home, I'll be home too. Have a great weekend! Be
good. You listen to T.J., Angela. He's in charge while I'm gone.
  Lots of love,
  Momma

Angela shoved a loaf of bread onto the counter and picked up Momma's phone. "She forgot her phone."

"No," T.J. said, feeling annoyed. "Angela, you didn't listen. She left it for us. So we can call her."

"That was dumb," said Angela. "If we call her, how can she answer? We have the phone. Duh!" Angela began pushing buttons on the cell phone, and it made tiny chirping sounds as if it were a small animal under attack. T.J. grabbed her hand and pried it from her fingers.

"Did you hear what Momma wrote about me being in charge?" T.J. asked. "And cut out that 'duh' stuff. Momma wants us to call her on Billy's phone."

"No way am I calling *Billy*!" Angela pulled a jar of may- onnaise from the refrigerator. "You want mustard?"

"No! Stop being so dense! Momma's *with* Billy."

"No, she's not. She wouldn't go off with *him*. No way."

"But she did! She's with Billy. She'll be back on Monday."

Angela shrugged and then seemed preoccupied with an armload of sandwich makings. Soon the counter was littered with bits of meat and cheese and smeared with mayonnaise. A pickle lay on the floor.

T.J. held the small phone in his hand, surprised at how cool it felt. He wasn't sure how to use it, but that shouldn't be too difficult to figure out, he thought. But he didn't want Angela playing with it or having a tantrum and tossing it into the toilet or out a window. This phone was their only link to their mother.

He knew better than to forbid Angela to touch it. That would be like an invitation to her to try to get hold of it again. He'd have to hide it while Angela was busy eating that pile of food she called a sandwich.

T.J. went into Momma's room. The bed was made, and the top of the dresser was nearly bare. He avoided looking in the closets, afraid they might be empty. He started toward the dresser, then changed his mind and put the phone in the drawer in the bedside table. There was a lot of junk in that drawer, which made him sigh with a degree of relief.

He wanted to call Momma right now. Tell her to come home. But he was afraid to call. Billy would probably answer. So, he decided, there was no point in calling at all.

The weekend went quickly, considering that they stayed inside, eating and watching TV. Momma had bought all sorts of wonderful food, things they had other times but never in such quantities and without Billy there to devour the hog share. Lots of sugary cereals with names like Chocolate Drop Crunchies and Sugar Plum Puffs. And the small freezer at the top of the refrigerator was stuffed with frozen dinners, not just macaroni and cheese, which was Angela's favorite, but chicken with rice and veggies and even lasagna. T.J. loved the meals with separate compartments. Some even had a place for a tiny dessert such as apple crisp or cherry cobbler.

They took turns digging through the freezer to find what they each wanted for lunch and dinner. Angela stood on a kitchen chair and several times dropped a cascade of packaged meals on the floor. But T.J. just wiped them off on his jeans and shoved them back in the freezer.

When Angela was busy watching cartoons or folding a

paper crane, he reread and reread Momma's note. He'd soon memorized the line where she told them, "Be sure to go to school on Monday, and when you get home, I'll be home too."

At first he found that reassuring, and he told himself over and over that Momma would be home on Monday.

It was when he was repeating that line to Angela on Sunday night that he realized what Momma must have forgotten. If *he* went to school, Angela would be home alone all Monday morning. No way could he trust Angela to get herself ready and out of the apartment and onto her school bus for afternoon kindergarten. Maybe he should call Momma and remind her of that fact. But if she'd already made her plans—plane tickets and all that stuff—she wouldn't be able to change things on such short notice.

Thinking about all of this made T.J. stop talking to Angela. He went into the kitchen and stared at the dirty bowls on the counter and the food-encrusted utensils in the sink. Momma should have bought a bunch of paper plates and bowls. This apartment didn't have a dishwasher, and he'd never realized how fast dishes and silverware could get used. Especially when he and Angela had been eating nonstop. The trash basket under the sink was half full with the plastic containers from the microwaved meals.

Angela had started jumping on the couch, but he wasn't looking. He could hear the sound of the cushions as they compressed, as if they were protesting. Sometimes ignoring Angela worked. This time she quit jumping because she threw up.

T.J. felt sick himself when he smelled and saw the mess on the same place where they usually slept.

"Get off!" he yelled. "You're gonna have to help me clean that up. I told you not to eat all that ice cream. You don't listen, Angela. Momma said I was in charge. That means you're supposed to do what I say."

Angela leaped off the couch, her hand over her mouth, and ran to the bathroom. T.J. got some paper towels and tried to clean up the vomit with one hand and hold his nose with the other.

That night they both avoided the living room and watched TV in Momma's room and slept in her bed. T.J. stayed awake late. He took the cell phone out of the nightstand and examined it, hoping that it would tell him he'd missed a call from Momma. But the phone held no messages. He slept with it in his hand, and when he woke up Monday morning it was still pressed against his palm, his fingers stiffly cradling the mute device.

Angela got up cranky. Her face looked dirty even though she'd taken a shower the night before. "Did Momma call?" she demanded.

"No, not yet."

"You should plug that phone in, T.J. It's going to go dead soon if you don't recharge it."

"Oh, yeah." He was embarrassed that he hadn't thought of that. He glanced around the bedroom.

"Over there, stupid," said Angela, pointing to the charger on top of the dresser. Then she headed for the bathroom.

T.J. plugged in the phone and watched the red light go on. His stomach growled, and he went to the kitchen to get out the cereal.

"Wash your face," he called to Angela.

"I don't have to. I washed it last night," Angela said as she came out of the bathroom.

"You can't go to school with dirt all around your mouth,

Angela. You ate something after your shower, didn't you?"

"I was hungry. I threw up all that food, and I woke up in the night and I was hungry. I ate those chocolates in that fancy box." Angela pointed to a decorated box lying on the floor next to the smelly couch. Billy had bought those candies for Momma about a week before.

"Those weren't for you," said T.J.

"Whatever!" Angela flounced into the kitchen and grabbed the box of Raving Raisin Cereal out of T.J.'s hand. "Where's a bowl?"

T.J. pointed to the dirty dishes.

Angela looked at him, frowning. "They're all dirty. Wash one for me."

"I'm not your servant, Angela. Wash your own bowl!"

He was surprised when she went to the sink and rinsed out a bowl and a spoon. She looked so small and thin, reaching up to turn off the water. He wished he'd done all the dishes the night before.

She surprised him again by getting dressed in clean jeans and a T-shirt and putting on her sneakers without help. He offered to brush her hair, but she insisted on doing it herself, and he didn't comment when she neglected to get out a snarl of tangles on the back of her head. He noticed that she'd cleaned her face too.

"The bus comes at 11:26," she told him, nodding toward the clock on the wall in the kitchen. "I mean that's when I gotta leave."

"I'll walk you down," he said.

"Nah." Angela shook her head and laughed. "Momma doesn't do that, T.J. I'm a big girl now. But she watches from the window."

"Okay. I'll see you after school. Don't miss the bus. I can't drive to school to pick you up."

"Stop teasing, T.J. You know Momma will be home before I get home."

"Yeah, sure. And, Angela, if anybody asks about me, just say I'm sick. I've got … a bad cold. Momma says she's taking me to the doctor if I'm not better by Friday."

"What? You talked to Momma!"

"No. *No,* Angela! I made that up so nobody from school will call or come snooping around. You gotta tell it like that. So Momma doesn't get in trouble. Okay?"

Angela glanced at the clock on the wall. "Okay." She nodded wisely, then added, "I can do something better. I'll go to the office and tell the lady that you're sick. I'll say Momma didn't have time to write a note. Yet. The office lady is nice. And she thinks I'm cute and 'just precious.'"

T.J. grinned. "Whatever," he said.

Angela smiled back at him and then suddenly ran over to him and gave him a quick hug. She swung her backpack in one hand as she left the apartment.

T.J. went to the window. There was no way he (or Momma, he realized) could see the corner where Angela waited for the bus. He swallowed the uneasy feeling that rose in his throat.

All afternoon T.J. kept glancing at the kitchen clock as he attempted to clean up the apartment. But when he heard a noise at the door at 3:39, he wasn't surprised that it was Angela, home from kindergarten. Not Momma, home from Las Vegas.

21

Each day that week was similar to Monday. Except for Friday. On Friday, Angela refused to go to school.

She lay in bed and cried. T.J. sat beside her, rubbing her back.

"Where's Momma? Call her, T.J. Tell her to come home. Immediately!"

T.J.'s throat hurt as he swallowed. He didn't want to tell Angela that he'd been crying too. He'd called Billy's number over and over, starting on Monday night. Each time a chirpy little voice said, "Please enjoy the music while your party is reached." But Billy never answered. Sometimes the phone went dead, as if someone had hung up. Other times that same artificial voice told T.J. to leave a message. And he did. At least ten times, he told Momma to please call. Or to please come home.

"Where's that stupid phone?" Angela sat up, scrubbing her wet eyes with the backs of her hands.

"Here," said T.J. "I'll call for you." He pressed the right buttons and handed the phone to Angela. Then he got up off the bed and went to the bathroom. When he came back, she had thrown the phone against the wall and gone back to crying. T.J. wasn't sure whether he should be thankful the phone had not broken.

That afternoon, when school had let out, T.J. and Angela walked to the small store two blocks away. He had decided it was best for them to stay inside during school hours so adults on the street wouldn't wonder why they weren't in class.

At the store they bought a carton of milk and a box of cereal. T.J. was surprised by the cost. On Wednesday he'd found a cup on a shelf in the kitchen with $17.94 in it and thought that was a lot of money. He'd used both front pockets of his jeans to carry it all. Now he realized it was nothing. Well, next to nothing.

He stared at the change the checkout girl had just given him. No way could he buy food for any length of time on the amount of money in his hand and in his pockets.

"Wait," he said to Angela as she started out of the store. Before they'd walked over, he'd told her that they were buying only cereal and milk. Absolutely nothing else.

Angela turned back toward him. Her mouth was set in a thin line. The pale skin of her face had a bluish cast from the fluorescent lights. Her eyes were hidden in the dark hollows of their sockets.

"Come back," T.J. told her. "I've got more money. Let's get some other stuff too."

He let her pick out a couple of bags of potato chips, two candy bars, and a small bottle of orange juice. After he'd paid and they were walking home, Angela tugged at his arm. He was using both hands to carry the one bag.

"Momma's not coming home," Angela said so softly that at first T.J. thought he'd imagined the words. "Is she?"

"I don't know."

"Why isn't she coming home?" Angela had managed to insert her hand under his arm and was hanging on.

"Something must have happened ... maybe something that's made it hard for her to come back."

"Like what?" Angela's voice was high-pitched but barely above a whisper.

A fine mist that wasn't quite fog covered the streets. The sidewalk was filmed with moisture. The dampness settled gently on Angela's hair and shone in the streetlights like tiny jewels. The air smelled of a city springtime, a mixture of exhaust, garbage, and damp dirt.

T.J. shrugged. The milk and orange juice were heavier than he'd expected, and he wished he'd asked for another bag when they bought the extra treats.

"I want Momma to come home," Angela said.

T.J. felt helpless and small. "Momma might not come back, Angela. She might be ... she could be ... dead or something."

"Dead? Like ... like that pigeon?"

T.J. had forgotten about the dead pigeon they'd seen lying on the sidewalk a few months before. Now he could picture it clearly. Its head had stayed at a strange angle when Angela had moved its body with the toe of her shoe.

"But you said that pigeon flew into a window." Angela's grip on T.J.'s arm tightened. "What happened to Momma?"

"Momma went to Las Vegas in a plane. She flew too." He regretted having voiced his fears aloud, but it was too late now.

"Did the plane crash?" Angela asked. "Did Momma die?"

T.J. shook his head. "I don't think a plane crashed. We'd have seen news about it on TV. But something must be wrong." His mouth felt dry despite the damp air.

Angela let go of his arm and ran ahead a few paces. Then she dropped back beside him. They walked faster and faster.

T.J. couldn't resist letting his eyes skim along the row of cars, checking Momma's parking space. Empty.

The outer door to the apartment was locked. Usually it wasn't, at least not during the day. So T.J. had to set the bag of food on the stoop and struggle to get his keys out to open the heavy door.

As he staggered inside, Angela ran past him and charged up the stairs. By the time he reached the second floor, she had climbed onto the horizontal portion of metal railing and was prancing along it like a tightrope walker.

"Fly away!" she cried dramatically as she dropped one of her crumpled paper birds down through the space between the railings.

"Get off!" T.J. screamed, dropping the bag of food and rushing to grab Angela. She leaped down before he got to her, giggling shrilly.

"Angela! You can't do stuff like that. You could fall." T.J. felt his voice shaking like his insides.

"I won't fall! I gotta go down and get my red crane. Let me go, T.J. You're hurting my arm!"

He followed her back down the stairs, and just as she picked up the red scrap of paper, he saw the shadowy form of a woman through the window of the outer door. He almost yelled, "Momma!" but stopped himself when he realized his mistake.

It was the mother of the upstairs girl. T.J. pushed the door open for her and saw the girl too, behind her mother. She was holding a little boy's hand. Her mother was carrying a bag of groceries, and she smiled and nodded at T.J. She said something that he couldn't understand.

The girl ducked her head shyly. "My mother says thank you for opening the door. She is glad it's finally locked. Not locked is not safe. But when it is locked, it is not so ... so convenient now."

"Yeah." T.J. nodded. "I know what you mean. I mean … what your mom means."

The girl nodded. "I'm sorry you've been sick."

"How did you know I was sick?"

"At school. My friend in your homeroom told me. Are you better now?"

"I'm okay."

They all started up the stairs with the girl's mother in the lead. T.J. found himself beside the girl, whose name he suddenly remembered was Iza. T.J. was startled when she began doing his "crazy steps" game.

She was still holding her brother's hand, and the little boy stopped on each step with both feet, but Iza's feet went up and down.

"How'd you—?" T.J. grinned at her.

"I learned this from you. From watching you," she said. Then she stopped and leaned toward him. Her mother had nearly reached the top of the first flight of stairs, and Angela was right behind her.

"Are you okay?" Iza asked in a low voice. "I mean …"

"Sure." T.J. didn't know exactly what she meant, but he suddenly wanted the conversation to end.

"I did the right thing?" Iza asked. "That night? Calling 911?" She was frowning.

"Yeah. Sure. Thanks." For some reason, T.J. felt embarrassed. But the girl's sudden bright smile dispelled the feeling. He grinned back at her.

"Race you," Iza said.

Side by side, doing T.J.'s crazy steps, they climbed to the second floor, where Angela was waiting, holding the abandoned bag of groceries.

Iza still clutched her little brother's hand. "See you later, T.J.,"' she said and then reached out and lightly touched the back of his hand.

"Yeah, Iza." He felt a tiny ping of happiness, knowing that she remembered his name. "Later," he whispered.

That night, while Angela was lying on Momma's bed, munching potato chips and watching a rerun of *Law and Order*, he pawed through the heap of dirty clothes they'd been shoving into a corner of the bedroom. It took until the next commercial before he found it in the back pocket of a pair of jeans. He pulled out the tiny card and pressed out the wrinkles between his thumb and fingers as he went into the kitchen.

A strange odor was coming from the wastebasket under the sink. He wondered what Angela had thrown in there, but decided not to check. He left the light off. The cell phone had its own special glow. Carefully, T.J. punched in the number on the business card.

The recorded voice was friendly, and he could picture the social worker's round, pleasant face as he left a message.

"This is T.J. Riley. I'm Angela's big brother. We need help. I think …" He hesitated and then said, "… our momma's dead."

"Momma's dead?" Angela had come quietly from the bedroom and was standing next to the couch, staring at him, her hand over her mouth as if to keep her question from escaping.

T.J. made a decision. "Yes, Momma's dead."

22

NOW—

"Dr. Angelo. Dr. Angelo. Please come to …"

T.J. stops listening before he hears where that doctor with the name sort of like Angela's is supposed to go.

The waiting room has gotten busy. Three men—T.J. realizes they are drunk—stand belligerently at the window in front of the registration desk. One is yelling and swearing at the receptionist.

A woman holding the hand of a small boy comes toward T.J.'s seat. She has long golden brown hair and looks enough like Momma to make him drop his gaze.

"Is this seat taken?" she asks, motioning toward the photo album.

T.J. shakes his head quickly and snatches the big book from the chair. He clutches it against his chest, feeling almost protective.

BETWEEN—

Marlene was interested in their life books. Well, not Angela's, since Mrs. Cox was never able to convince Angela to make one. But Marlene sat with T.J. in those first days after they'd moved into the big house with her and Dan. Together, they looked through "My Life Book." Marlene acted truly interested, just as Mrs. Cox had predicted. She didn't ask too many questions and didn't say she thought his artwork was lame. Despite her low-key manner, T.J. felt tense, and sure enough, after they closed the cover, Marlene looked at him with a slightly wrinkled brow. He could tell she wanted to give him a hug, so he deliberately looked at the floor and stiffened his body.

Marlene sighed and asked, "So, do you want to talk about your birth mother? Or anything about your other life?"

T.J. wasn't sure how to answer. He took the safe route. "No."

THEN—

By the time Marlene and Dan started the process to adopt them, he and Angela hadn't seen Momma in a long time. Going on two years. During that time they'd lived in three or maybe four different foster homes that T.J. could not remember clearly. They didn't stay long in any one home.

There was always a very good reason for him and Angela to move. The foster family decided to relocate to another state. The mother was getting old and needed some sort of surgery. The family decided to adopt some of their foster kids who were not T.J. and Angela.

"It's not your fault. Just bad luck," Mrs. Cox said apologetically each time they were shuffled into another family.

He could recall small details about each of the foster homes, but the correct order ... he couldn't be sure. His memories of their time in foster care were jumbled up in his head like the letter squares of a Scrabble game, dumped together in a bag.

He thought they were living in the second foster home when Momma finally called.

"T.J.! How could you tell those AFCS people that I was dead? *Dead!*"

She sounded so close. Not as if she was in California, where the police—or maybe Mrs. Cox—had tracked her down.

"I *thought* you were dead," T.J. whispered. Angela was engrossed in a computer game in the next room, but he had to keep his voice down—he didn't want her to realize he was talking to their mother. "You didn't answer the phone. You didn't answer the messages I left." T.J.'s throat felt scratchy and his head hurt.

"Oh, T.J., I'm so sorry." Momma's voice was suddenly low and hoarse. "I should have called." She was quiet for a moment and then went on, talking quickly. "But Billy's phone got stolen while we were in Las Vegas. We got robbed. Talk about ironic!"

"Momma ..."

"You should see Las Vegas, T.J. What a place!"

"So, when are you coming home?"

"I don't know yet, T.J. Everything has gotten sort of complicated. Makes it impossible for me to get back there. I'm sorry."

"Impossible?"

"At this point, yes, impossible. The circumstances are just ... I can't explain it all. Not right now. But I can't leave California for a while. And see, I thought for sure my mother—Grandma—would step up and take care of you and Angela. I never wanted you kids to end up back in foster care."

T.J. moved across the room so Angela definitely couldn't hear him. He spoke softly. "Our caseworker, Mrs. Cox, told us Grandma wanted us to live with her. But Grandpa had a heart attack, and he's still in really bad shape. When he's better, we can go visit them. But we can't ... you know ... live there." That familiar pain was lodged in his belly.

"I know. I know. They told me. Those AFCS people said Dad is on oxygen. That Mom is overwhelmed, and it's no place for kids. Still ... you'd think she'd see it in her heart to help her own grandkids. I mean, *I* can't help it ..." Momma sounded as if she was talking more to herself than to him.

"Whatever," T.J. said, letting the bitterness slip out in that one word.

"I *said* I was sorry, T.J. It's not *my* fault I have such bad luck. Get Angela on the phone now."

At that moment, behind Momma's voice, in the background, he heard someone saying, "Celia, hurry up."

The voice was Billy's, T.J. thought. Or maybe someone like him.

T.J. swallowed hard. "Angela's busy. Bye, Momma."

She called again, just twice, while they were in foster care. But T.J. was lucky because Angela was asleep for one call and shopping with the foster mom for the other. During one of those phone conversations, Momma promised she'd come back and they'd be a family again, but T.J. waited and waited, and she didn't return. Even when Mrs. Cox said Momma was scheduled to come just for a visit, it didn't happen.

Angela asked T.J. about Momma off and on. But he kept repeating that she was dead, hoping Angela would forget that their mother had chosen Billy over them.

And then Mrs. Cox began explaining to them about being adopted. About a permanent home for the two of them. Together. Without Momma. Mrs. Cox said she'd talked to Momma and that Momma wanted to be with them but all sorts of things were going wrong in California and she couldn't seem to get it together.

"I'd like you two to have a *real* home soon," Mrs. Cox said.

Not a foster home. A "real" home. T.J. thought that was a funny way of saying it. Did that mean the house they were living in at that time, another foster home, was "pretend"?

"We live in a pretend house," he told Angela, because she loved things pretend. She pretended that her paper birds had names, that they were alive and needed to be fed. That they could really fly away. He made up a story and told it at bedtime to Angela and a couple of other foster kids. In his story, they all lived in a pretty, pretend house with a pointed roof and high, open windows so pretend paper cranes could fly away ... and come back.

Then one day Mrs. Cox arrived at the foster home with a huge smile on her face. She said she had important news. That Momma had made a "momentous and difficult" decision. That a judge had been involved too, somehow. That Momma had signed a bunch of papers.

"Your birth mother just can't cope with everything," Mrs. Cox told them. "She's decided that the best thing for her to do—for your sakes—is to relinquish her rights. She wants us—me and the department—to make an adoption plan for the two of you."

Angela leaned her elbows on the table and began to suck her thumb. She rolled her eyes at T.J. as if to say, *You* tell her.

"We thought ..." T.J. hesitated. "We think our mother's dead."

Mrs. Cox frowned. "I know. I've heard that from your foster parents. But she's not dead or I wouldn't have her signature on this." She pulled out a sheet of paper. "See? Celia Riley."

T.J. stared at the rounded cursive. He glanced at Angela. She disengaged her thumb to mouth *Whatever* at him.

Mrs. Cox returned the paper to its place and smiled at him and then Angela. "You do understand the difference between foster care and adoption, right?"

T.J. nodded. He noticed, out of the corner of his eye, that Angela was imitating him.

In a way, all of this made sense to T.J., but it didn't make *any* sense to Angela, who told T.J. after Mrs. Cox drove away, "She's lying. Momma's dead. If she was alive, she'd come for us. Wouldn't she, T.J.?"

"Yeah."

"Momma didn't sign anything," said Angela. "She's dead."

NOW—

T.J. squirms on the chair he's been sitting in for so long. He opens his life book one more time and makes himself turn past several blank pages that Marlene suggested he save for later. "For when you want to add something. Something more about your other life."

He's never going to do that. As far as T.J. is concerned, his life book is finished. He wants those blank pages to stay that way.

The rest of the album is filled with pictures of what Marlene and Dan call their "new life."

BETWEEN—

Marlene sat down with him about a month ago and showed him a whole array of snapshots that she and Dan had taken since the day they'd met him and Angela. She spread the photos out on the coffee table and asked him to help pick the ones he wanted to add to his life book.

T.J. knew how much Marlene loved to make scrapbooks. In the family room of this big suburban house was a special shelf full of clearly labeled scrapbooks that chronicled Marlene and Dan's life. T.J. and Angela had seen some of

those scrapbooks—beautifully arranged photos with decorated paper backgrounds and neatly lettered notes under or
beside each picture: *Our trip to Yellowstone. Dan and Bowser
at the lake. Marlene, learning to paddle a canoe. Camping in
the Black Hills.*

The picture of Bowser showed a dog with a dark head
and lighter markings that made it look as if he was wearing
a mask. Marlene had gotten tears in her eyes when T.J. asked
about the dog.

"He died a month before we heard about you and Angela.
He was a great dog." Marlene smiled at T.J. "We decided to
wait a while to get another dog. Then we got the best, most
exciting news. We were going to be parents! We're still planning to get a dog, after you kids are a bit more settled. But
Bowser—he was special. I guess he was our baby for those
thirteen years we had him."

T.J. wasn't quite sure what Marlene meant about a dog
being a baby, especially not a dog that was thirteen. But he
nodded. It was peaceful, sitting on the couch with Marlene,
looking through pictures that never showed anyone being hurt
or cursing or having a tantrum. Or leaving and not coming
back.

So he didn't resist her helping him put the newer photos
in "My Life Book." Marlene called these snapshots "family
photos." She liked to use the word "family" a lot.

NOW—

T.J. runs his fingers lightly over the plastic covering on the
page in front of him. Beneath the plastic is an arrangement of
pictures taken on the day he and Angela first met Marlene and
Dan. T.J. frowns. He was wearing that stupid red cap with

the green stripes. Angela looks surprisingly small in these pictures, taken over a year ago.

The next page is labeled *Family Fun*, and is crowded with snapshots of all four of them. Marlene and T.J. playing catch with a huge yellow ball in the yard. Angela on a pony at the county fair. T.J. and Dan tossing a football. All four of them smiling and holding up pumpkins.

There are more pages, dedicated to special occasions. Their first Thanksgiving at their new grandparents' house. Christmas. Angela's eighth birthday. T.J.'s twelfth birthday. Adoption Day (although Marlene has been working on a whole special scrapbook dedicated to that day).

The final page shows two pictures that he chose from the pile Marlene offered.

One snapshot is of himself, looking tall, one foot resting on a soccer ball. The day it was taken, Dan was showing him how to dribble and trap a ball. T.J. was toying with the idea of trying out for the community soccer team in the spring.

Now, as he sits in the waiting room, he can't make himself think that far ahead.

The other picture is of Angela. It was taken on her eighth birthday. She's standing in front of a huge birdcage, a bright green parakeet perched on one finger. Angela is grinning at the camera. Behind her T.J. can see part of the hallway that leads to the staircase. He can almost see in the photo the spot where she fell this morning.

Now he gently shuts the life book and squeezes his eyes closed too. He is trying to see paper birds, flying back like tiny, bright-colored homing pigeons. Instead he sees Angela— one arm flung out, fingers spread wide, hair swept upward. Angela, falling.

23

Today started out like any other Saturday morning. T.J. and Angela watched cartoons in the family room until Marlene came down and made breakfast.

They all ate together at the large round table in the kitchen. Dan was still looking sleepy, although he'd had his shower and his wet hair was lined with marks from the teeth of a comb. He'd been up late Friday night, working on some problem with the computer located in his upstairs den. T.J. thought it was strange for someone whose job involved working on computers all day to spend hours on a computer at home.

Angela was looking grumpy because Marlene had insisted that the TV in the family room be turned off.

"Why?" Angela wanted to know. "If we keep it turned up loud, I can hear it and still eat at the table." After a year of being part of this family, both Angela and T.J. knew Marlene was not a big fan of TV. And there was no way she would tolerate it being on all day. In their other life, the TV had been on nearly nonstop. T.J. still missed the comforting background noise and guessed that his sister did too.

"I just want a family breakfast, Angela. At the table. With quiet so we can all talk to one another and hear what we're saying." Marlene was taking a pan out of the oven.

The scent of freshly baked cinnamon rolls made T.J.'s mouth water. Angela slouched in her chair and began sucking her thumb.

T.J. saw a flicker of annoyance on Marlene's face when

she glanced at Angela, but she said nothing as she flipped the pan. The rolls tumbled into a big ceramic bowl on the counter.

Suddenly the parakeet began squawking.

Dan laughed easily. "I guess Polly wants to make sure she's heard too."

"Oh, Dan ..." Marlene said.

"Her name is not Polly!" Angela almost yelled.

"Well, what is her name?" Dan was swooping up the bowl of cinnamon rolls and placing it on the table.

Angela stuck her thumb back in her mouth and scowled at him.

"You know, Angela," Dan continued in a good-natured tone, "for someone who kept asking for a green parakeet, you haven't shown much interest in her. She's probably trying to tell you to pay attention to her."

"Whatever," Angela said with a roll of her eyes.

"That's enough." Marlene's voice was firm.

T.J.'s stomach tightened. It was better to just ignore Angela when she was in a bad mood, but Marlene didn't seem to realize that.

"You can take it back," Angela said.

"What?" Marlene asked the question, but Dan turned toward Angela and stared as if he couldn't quite believe his ears.

"That dumb bird. Take it back to the pet store." Angela shoved a too-big bite of cinnamon roll into her mouth.

Marlene and Dan exchanged looks. T.J. knew they had not wanted to get a bird in the first place, but Mrs. Cox—and the family therapist they all visited once a month—had thought it was a good idea. T.J. had overheard a conversation between Marlene and Mrs. Cox about how a real bird might help Angela get over her obsession with making paper cranes.

"It doesn't even talk," Angela said. "I thought it would talk. And I wanted to let it fly around. Free. But *you* won't let me take it out of that dumb cage."

"That dumb cage is gigantic, and it cost a small fortune," said Dan.

"Let's just eat," said Marlene, sounding tired. She put a heap of scrambled eggs on each plate. T.J. took a mouthful and drank a huge gulp of orange juice to help wash down the eggs.

Dan glanced at Marlene and frowned, then turned back to Angela. "I told you yesterday that we'd start letting her out in the family room in a few weeks. She needs time to get used to us."

Angela shrugged. "I don't want it."

Dan sighed. "I thought all along we should get a dog. Or a puppy."

Or a kitten, T.J. thought. An image from his "other life" of a soft gray kitten suddenly appeared in his mind's eye.

"Whatever," Angela said again.

Marlene said, "I don't like that expression, Angela, and you know it."

Which is exactly why she's using it, thought T.J.

"T.J. says 'whatever' all the time," countered his sister.

"Please call him Timothy," Marlene said, replaying a request she'd made over and over in the past year.

"Well," said Dan, "I can see it was very worthwhile to turn off the TV and have this pleasant conversation. But I have better things to do." He stood up, collected his empty cup and plate, and took them to the sink.

"Dan, please don't be sarcastic." Marlene blinked, and T.J. wasn't surprised to see tears in her eyes.

"I'm sorry, honey."

"Dan, please stay," Marlene said.

"Honey, I didn't get much sleep last night." Dan ran water over his dishes. "I just don't feel up to participating in—or listening to —another 'discussion.' I'll come back down in a bit and load the dishwasher."

It was the therapist who'd suggested that they all "reframe" what they'd been calling "arguments" and call them "discussions."

Dan circled the table to rub the top of T.J.'s head, give Marlene a quick kiss, and hold one hand up to Angela, who refused to give him a high-five.

"Okay," Marlene said softly. "You kids finish your food and clear your places, and you can go turn on the TV."

Dan retreated to his computer room upstairs and Marlene began rinsing off the remaining dishes.

"Stupid bird," Angela said as she walked into the family room and kicked the base of the cage. The parakeet fluttered wildly and made loud squawks of complaint.

"Angela!" Marlene yelled. "What is wrong with you? You'll scare that poor bird to death."

Angela flapped her arms and addressed the parakeet. "Dumb bird! Stupiotic!" Then she swooped in a circle, waving her arms and chirping.

"Stop acting 'stupiotic' yourself," T.J. said as he flopped onto the couch.

Marlene was now standing next to the birdcage, her hands on her hips. "You need to take care of this parakeet, young lady. Did you check its water this morning?"

"I. Don't. Want. It." Angela flung herself onto the couch and grabbed the remote. She managed to turn on the TV and increase the volume at the same time. The noise was so loud it hurt.

"Turn that off," Marlene ordered.

"No!" Angela screamed, but T.J. wrestled the remote from her hand and hit "mute."

"That's better." Marlene came into the room and sat between them on the couch. "Now, Angela, tell me why you don't want that poor bird."

Angela was sucking her thumb and glaring at the silent TV.

"Just tell her, Angela," T.J. said, although he had no idea why Angela had changed her mind. He suspected that the whole anti-parakeet argument was more about the non-TV-watching breakfast than any real dislike of the bird.

Angela shook her head and sucked audibly.

"Please," T.J. whispered. "Pretty please with strawberries and whipped cream and chocolate sauce and coconut and ..."

"No coconut, stupid. I *hate* coconut." Angela had pulled her thumb plug out of her mouth and now stuck out her tongue at T.J. There was a hint of a grin on her face.

"Okay, whatever," said T.J.

"See? I told you T.J. says 'whatever' all the time."

"I see what you mean," said Marlene, smiling. "We'll have to work on that. But I'd still really, really like to know why you've decided you don't want your parakeet."

Angela looked at T.J. He nodded encouragingly.

"Because birds die," Angela said. "Daddy told me yesterday. He said Chartreuse would *die* if I didn't take care of her. Like that pigeon we found. Remember, T.J.? It was dead. Like Momma."

"Oh, honey." Marlene sighed and tried to put her arm around Angela's shoulders.

But Angela shrugged and got up off the couch. "I don't want a *dead* bird."

"Your parakeet will live a long time," Marlene said. "Daddy just wanted you to understand that you need to take good care of her. And we're always here to help you."

T.J. nodded again, hoping the discussion was about to end. Angela turned to look across the room at Chartreuse in her cage.

"And, Angela," Marlene continued, "you know your birth mother is *not* dead. We've talked about that before."

T.J. knew Marlene should have quit talking. He squinted at the cartoon characters that were racing back and forth across the silent screen.

Angela stamped her foot and yelled at Marlene, "She's dead!" Then she ran from the room and up the stairs.

Marlene leaned back and rubbed her forehead. "I don't know what to say sometimes, Timothy." She put her arms out, asking for a hug.

Something hard inside T.J. made him say, without even thinking, "My name's not Timothy." He stood up, dropped the remote on the couch, and followed his sister upstairs.

He went into his own room and looked around. Except for being sort of messy, it could have been used for a picture in a furniture catalog. Along one wall was a bunk bed with Spider-Man comforters for both the top and the bottom. In front of the window were a gigantic desk and a lamp with a bright blue shade. A red bookshelf held a small library. The rug was striped red, white, and blue.

He had an overwhelming sense that he did not belong in this room—this place—where he was called Timothy.

Funny thing. Downstairs, a few minutes before, was the

first time he'd said anything about his name to Marlene in all those months of living here. Angela always called him T.J., and Dan sometimes did too. But Marlene was determined. She seemed to think that if she called him Timothy, he'd *be* Timothy. He wondered if Mrs. Cox had ever told Marlene and Dan that he was not Timothy James. That he was just T.J. Maybe she forgot.

He climbed into the top bunk and lay back, staring at the pale blue ceiling. When they first moved in, Marlene had asked him if he wanted her to paint clouds on the ceiling, but he had told her no.

Clouds were for girls. But now he wished for clouds.

He shut his eyes. He thought he heard someone going down the stairs, but he didn't move.

The next thing he heard was Angela screaming. "My birds! Give 'em back!"

T.J. sat up in bed. The voices were coming from the family room downstairs. His room was the closest to the top of the steps, so he could hear Marlene's answer clearly.

"Angela! I've told you *not* to get into my scrapbooking supplies! That paper isn't for origami birds. It's for scrapbook pages. You have a whole drawer full of origami paper. I've told you before. Any birds made from Mommy's paper belong to me."

"No! Mine!" Angela sounded like a two-year-old. T.J. began chewing on a fingernail.

"Angela! Stop hitting! That hurts! Do not hit your mother!"

"You're not my momma. You can't tell me what to do! My *real* mother's dead!"

"Okay, Angela." Marlene's voice was weary and sad. "You can have these paper birds back. But I want you to listen to me."

There was a moment of complete quiet. T.J. swung his legs over the side of the bed.

"Your birth mother is alive and living in California."

"No, she's not. T.J. told me she's dead!"

Marlene's voice got softer. "Your birth mother can't take care of you, Angela. She's not dead. Mrs. Cox talked to you about all that. And Mrs. Cox helped us to meet you and Timothy. When you first came here, you were still foster kids. But then we officially adopted you. You remember Adoption Day in September."

T.J. thought she was overdoing the adoption thing and could imagine Angela covering her ears by now. But Marlene kept talking as if Angela was a first grader or a slow learner.

"We went to court and you met that nice judge. It's all legal now. Dan's your dad, and I am your mom. That's why you live with Dan and me, now. And Timothy."

"My momma's dead!" Angela yelled, and then T.J. heard her come tearing up the stairs. He caught a glimpse of her as she flashed past his open door, heading down the hallway to her room. Then he heard her scream, "And his name's T.J. Just T.J.!"

He flopped back on the bed. Leave it to Angela to pick up on something that would make Marlene even more upset. Next Marlene would go tell Dan, who must have the door to his den shut or he'd have heard all that yelling.

Or maybe Dan was hiding, like T.J. Both of them trying to find a piece of quiet. That thought almost made him smile.

He lay still, listening for a few minutes. He heard the radio in the kitchen being turned up, so Marlene must have gone in there and decided to ignore Angela.

T.J. jumped down off the top bunk and went to the bathroom.

It was after he came out and was crossing the hallway to go back to his room that he saw Angela.

She was walking toward him on the wooden railing that ran along one side of the hallway. She held her arms outstretched for balance, and her feet were bare. In each hand she clutched a paper crane.

T.J. squinted against the sunlight that flooded through the window at the other end of the hallway. The light turned each wavy strand of Angela's hair to white gold. And he could see the intricate designs on the paper she'd used to make the birds. Marlene's scrapbook paper.

On one side of the banister was a two-and-a-half-foot drop to the floor of the upstairs hallway. On the other side was a narrow open space and a twelve-foot drop to the downstairs floor.

He felt a sick wave of apprehension. "Get down, Angela!"

"No! I'm setting my birds free!" Angela dropped one of the scrapbook birds into the open space.

"Those birds are just paper," said T.J.

"They're real! And they can't die!" Another bird fell from her hand.

T.J. was stumped for a moment by her logic. "Okay, they can't die, but that's because they're not alive."

"Duh!" Angela stuck out her tongue, then reached into her pocket for another paper bird. "Momma *was* alive," she said. "*Now* she's dead. That's why she never came back."

T.J. stepped toward his sister, trying to gauge if he could

grab her off the railing without knocking her into that open space. "Angela, *everybody*'s been telling you that Momma's still alive."

"No! *You* told me she's dead!" Angela flung a crumpled bird into the void.

He knew he should shut up. The important thing was to get his sister off the railing.

But suddenly he wanted her to admit the truth. He was sick of pretending, sick of protecting her. He wanted her to feel the way he did about Momma—hurt, sad, and angry.

"She's alive," he said.

"I'm. Not. Listening!" Angela stopped walking and covered her ears with her hands. Then she tried to turn around on the wooden railing.

"Don't!" T.J. realized she couldn't keep her balance without holding out her arms. Angela's bare feet slipped as she made a stumbling step. For a moment T.J. thought she would topple onto the floor three feet in front of him. But instead her body tilted toward the open space. She jerked her hands off her ears. Too late.

T.J. reached out, but she was already falling.

He saw her hit the floor with a solid thud. She didn't move.

24

"Are you asleep, Timothy?"

His head jerks upright as if it's attached to strings that have been pulled. Marlene is kneeling in front of him. The skin of her face looks gray and tight.

"What? What's happened?" he asks.

"You can come with me now. She's been moved to the PIC Unit. Pediatric Intensive Care. They said you could see her. For just a few minutes. Even though ... even though there's no change."

"Does that mean she's going to die?" There. He said it.

Marlene touches his shoulder as he scrambles to his feet. "They keep monitoring her—something about pressure in her brain ... I can't ..." Her voice dissolves into a murmur he can't understand.

T.J. grabs his life book and follows Marlene out of the waiting room and along a corridor to an elevator. He expected to go through those wide swinging doors into the Emergency Room, and feels vaguely cheated and disoriented.

The elevator makes a soft humming noise and smells faintly of perfume. It's a scent that reminds him of Momma, and he imagines, for just a moment, that her ghost is in that elevator with him.

They get off on the fourth floor. Marlene walks so fast that he has no time to think. As they go around a corner, Dan steps from an alcove and takes Marlene's arm.

"No change," Dan says. "I just needed a bathroom break."

They stop at some large doors. Dan pushes a button on the wall, and a squeaky voice asks, "May I help you?"

"We're Angela Westel's parents. And her brother."

"Come in," says the voice, followed by a buzzing sound, and the three of them go through the doors.

Together they approach a large desk area with nurses and monitors. T.J. hangs back, feeling nervous. Out of the corner of an eye he sees glassed-in rooms, each with a small bed or a crib. He tries not to look, but still he catches glimpses of tiny hands with wires or tubes coming out of them, bandaged legs, a dark head with a metal halo, a tent-like enclosure with a little boy, nearly naked, breathing so hard his whole chest sinks in. He hears hissing and soft beeping noises and several children crying fitfully, and he feels the hairs on his arms rising. T.J. longs to retreat to the familiar waiting room.

He follows Dan and almost collides with him when he stops in front of one of those windowed rooms.

"Don't be upset," Dan says softly. "It looks kind of scary because they've got her hooked up to some machines. All sorts of equipment to monitor her vital signs and stuff, so they can keep track of how she's doing."

"Mr. and Mrs. Westel?" A doctor is approaching from the side. One arm is extended as if he wants to shake Dan's hand or maybe restrain him. "I just want to do a quick check," he says brusquely. He opens the door to Angela's room, and they all follow him in.

She's in a bed, not a crib, T.J. notes with some satisfaction. Angela would be upset if they had put her in a crib.

"Is there any change?" Dan is whispering.

The doctor doesn't answer as he expertly pries Angela's

eyelids up, one at a time, and shines a tiny beam of light into her pupils. T.J.'s legs feel weak, as if he's been sick.

Finally, the doctor turns from Angela and says quietly, "We have to be patient. She seems to be showing some signs of coming around. But with a concussion this bad, we just don't know. The fact that she's young is in her favor. I'll be back again soon."

Then he's gone, leaving the three of them to arrange themselves around Angela's bed, which T.J. now decides looks way too big for her eight-year-old body. Dan scoots chairs up close to the bed, and T.J. places his life book on the floor beneath a chair and sits down.

Marlene strokes Angela's arm, the one without the IV tube stuck into it. T.J. thinks about tickling her toes, but they are hidden under the sheet.

"Angela," he says, and he thinks her eyelids flutter. *Please wake up. Pretty please with piles of coconut …*

A young nurse comes into the room. "I need to draw some blood. They want to run another test. It'll just take a sec."

Dan turns his head away, and Marlene stares at Angela's small, pale face. T.J. watches the needle go into the soft skin of Angela's arm and sees the transparent vial turn red. There's an angry bruise above her elbow.

He sees her hand twitch. "Ouch. Stop. That. Hurts." Angela's eyes are open.

"Sorry," says the nurse. "Welcome to the PIC Unit, Angie."

"My name's Angela."

The nurse smiles. "Good! That's great. I'm going to go get Dr. Hartman and tell him you're awake."

When the nurse leaves, Angela looks around the room. Her cheeks have suddenly turned bright pink like her princess doll's.

"Hi, T.J.," she says hoarsely, as if her voice has gotten rusty.

T.J. expects Marlene to correct Angela, to say, "Call him *Timothy*," but instead she lifts Angela's arm and kisses her hand. "Welcome back, Angela," she whispers.

"What's wrong with Daddy?" Angela asks.

Dan has gone into a curtained corner of the room, and T.J. can see his back, his shoulders hunched and heaving. Dan is crying.

T.J. feels something inside that he can't identify or describe. Tears fill his own eyes, and he needs a tissue badly.

"Daddy," says Marlene, "is just so glad you are waking up. And I'm glad too, and so is … T.J."

Angela tries to sit up. "Ow! My arm hurts. And my head. What happened? Why am I here?"

Dr. Hartman has stepped into the room, a relieved smile on his face. "Good questions, young lady. But your family can answer them better than I can."

"Don't call me 'young lady,'" Angela says. "That's what Mommy calls me when she's mad at me."

The doctor gives a satisfied nod, as if Angela has just passed a major exam.

"I'd like to talk with your parents, Angela, for a few minutes, out there by that big desk. Just lie there and relax. We're going to keep you here for a couple of days until we're sure your head is okay. Your brother can stay with you for a while."

As soon as Marlene and Dan leave with the doctor, Angela reaches for T.J.'s hand. Her fingers feel cold and dry. "What happened?"

"You really don't remember?"

"No. I … Did we watch cartoons today? Is it Saturday?"

"Yeah, it's Saturday." T.J. thinks of all the bad memories he'd like to erase from their other life. And this one bad memory from their new life. "You fell off the upstairs railing at Dan and Marlene's house. At home. You fell because I … I was telling you … something you didn't want to hear. And you put your hands over your ears."

"What didn't I want to hear?"

"Our momma's not dead. She's alive and living in California."

"Oh." Angela pulls her hand from his and begins to suck her thumb.

T.J. sits and listens to the small, strange noises of the hospital machines. Angela turns slightly away from him.

"Ow. My head hurts, and my thumb tastes weird."

"Probably it turned to coconut while you were knocked out."

"Yeah. I hate coconut."

"I know."

T.J. shifts his position just enough to see the nurses' station through the windowed wall of Angela's room. He can see Dr. Hartman talking to Dan and Marlene, who are standing close together, their arms around each other, heads bent forward in concentration. He knows they are going to do whatever the doctor prescribes to help Angela recover from her injuries.

"So," Angela says in her rusty voice, "you lied to me. Before? When you said Momma was dead?"

"Yeah."

"Why?"

"At first, I *thought* she was dead. Maybe. And when she didn't come back, it was like she *was* dead. And I didn't want you to know that she didn't want us. So then it was easier to … to pretend she was dead."

Easier. Momma often lied because it was easier.

Angela looks up at T.J. and says, "It should be a good thing, though, right? I mean, our momma being alive?"

T.J. blinks back more tears as he looks at his sister. He is so glad she woke up.

"Yeah," T.J. whispers. "It's good, Momma being alive."

"You wanna know something?" Angela asks. "The real truth and nothing but the truth?"

T.J. shrugs, not sure.

"The thing is … the truth is, T.J., I don't remember our momma that much. Was she—is she pretty?"

"See for yourself." T.J. reaches beneath the chair, pulls out his life book, and pries it open to the picture of Momma. He holds the big photo album up in front of Angela's face. "See? She's beautiful. Just like you, Angela."

"Thanks, T.J." She shuts her eyes.

T.J. puts his life book back under his chair.

He imagines Dan and Marlene returning and him telling them why Angela fell. He knows he'll get a lecture from Dan about being more responsible and a tearful hug from Marlene that will mean he's forgiven.

T.J. realizes that he likes knowing what to expect. He expects other things, too. Like Dan and Marlene keeping that green parakeet, and Angela, someday, maybe, teaching it to talk. He expects that they'll get him a kitten or a puppy if he asks for one. But most of all, he simply expects Dan and Marlene to be there for him and Angela.

He imagines someone, maybe that young nurse, taking a picture of the four of them, Dan, Marlene, Angela, and him, right here in Angela's hospital room. Marlene will use that picture in one of her scrapbooks. She'll label it *Our Family: When Angela Woke Up.*

T.J. rubs his eyes. Another letter to Momma writes itself in his mind. But this time he will put it on paper, and he'll ask Marlene to help him find a way to make sure Momma gets it.

Dear Momma,
  How are you? I am fine. So is Angela.
    Love,
    T.J. a.k.a. Timothy